GERT GARIBALDI'S
RANTS AND RAVES

One Butt Cheek at a Time

also by amber kizer

MERIDIAN

GERT GARIBALDI'S
RANTS AND RAVES

One Butt Cheek at a Time

amber kizer

DELACORTE PRESS

Copyright © 2007 by Amber Kizer

All rights reserved. Published in the United States by Delacorte Press, an imprint of Random House Children's Books, a division of Random House, Inc., New York. Originally published in hardcover in the United States by Delacorte Press in 2007.

Delacorte Press is a registered trademark and the colophon is a trademark of Random House, Inc.

Visit us on the Web! www.randomhouse.com/teens

Educators and librarians, for a variety of teaching tools, visit us at www.randomhouse.com/teachers

The Library of Congress has cataloged the hardcover edition of this work as follows:

Kizer, Amber.
Gert Garibaldi's rants and raves : one butt cheek at a time / by Amber Kizer.
p. cm.
Summary: An intelligent but insecure high school sophomore shares her private thoughts about sexy boys, her aged parents, annoying teachers, and growing up.
ISBN: 978-0-385-73430-1 (trade)
ISBN: 978-0-385-90439-1 (library)
ISBN: 978-0-375-89061-1 (e-book)
[1. High schools—Fiction. 2. Schools—Fiction. 3. Humorous stories.] I. Title.
PZ7.K6745Ge 2007
[Fic]—dc22
2007002410

ISBN: 978-0-385-73431-8 (tr. pbk.)

Printed in the United States of America

10 9 8 7 6 5 4 3 2 1

First Trade Paperback Edition

To my own personal Pollyanna, who played the glad game even in my darkest hours, when we had no idea what the future might hold. Thanks for remembering I could do this on the days when I forgot. You make life with pain bearable.

I couldn't do it without you.

Thank you, Mom.

Special thanks to Rosie Donnelly, whose invitation to join the teachers' workshop opened the world of writing to me. Couldn't have done it without that opportunity, thank you! Thanks to Mary Bakeman, who read this multiple times and always had time to edit. To Randayle Greyson, critique partner extraordinaire—no wannabes for us! Peter Kizer, thanks, Dad, for "you said, I suggest"; the line-by-line was hugely helpful. Rosemary Stimola, the best agent ever! Thanks! Stephanie Lane, thank you for your vision and for sharpening Gert's world. And for handing her the box of tissues when she was trying to get away with sarcasm rather than emotion. Kenny Holcomb, thank you for an inspired book design. And Sarah LaMar for the best pictures ever—you've got talent, girl!

the butt cheek
philosophy of life

My parents always say, "Put one foot in front of the other." What is that? It's discriminatory, for one thing. Not everyone has feet, nor can everyone move their feet. But here's the epiphany that is my brilliance—we all have butts. Seriously, even people without legs and arms have butts, right?

Okay, so survival isn't about putting a foot in front of your trunk and shuffling along. Nope. It's about moving the butt cheeks and getting them into the pants of life. It's my philosophy of attacking life, or more accurately, surviving life's attacks on me. Has been since I was little, when my tush was an adorable twin set of dumplings, so forever and ever, A-WOMEN.

I get up, find the pants for the day that fit my butt and wiggle into them. One. Butt. Cheek. At. A. Time. One and then the other. Simple. Deceptively simple. Eventually, because some days it takes longer than others, I get both cheeks into the jeans and life doesn't feel quite so overwhelming.

It's little things that add up to the big things. So try it. The next time you don't think you can get out of bed or tackle the next obstacle, just focus on your butt and your jeans. One cheek up, then the other. And you're ready to go. It works, trust me. It's gotten me this far.

one

Okay, so here's the deal. My best friend's Adam. Adam Bryant. No, this isn't one of those disgustingly sweet stories about how best friends figure out by senior prom that they're deeply in love and can't live without each other.

Yuck. Has that ever happened in real life? Uh, no. Anyway, Adam likes Tim, so it would never work. I'm a girl, he's a boy, we both like boys, you get the idea.

And no, we're not those two small-town teens who move to the big city to find ourselves at the bottom of a beer can, with an MTV sound track and tons of making out with strangers. We don't fit here, but honestly, can we fit anywhere? I don't know yet. I'll keep you posted.

Tangent: sorry.

The point is, I like Tim's twin brother, Lucas. Lucas is in third-period English with me. He's a junior, but I'm a Brain sophomore, so it evens out. We don't really know each other. And he's tight with the in crowd, which means the people he talks to are *not* the same people I talk to. I mean, if I'm honest, Tim and I have many more conversations than me and Lucas. I say hi in the halls and, if Lucas isn't busy with someone else, he sometimes says hi back. But I'm optimistic. It's only a matter of time before he figures out we're perfect for each other.

English isn't the most romantic place to have a crush. It's not drama, where you can hide in dark costume closets, or bio, where you can snuggle around the Bunsen burner.

You know what I'm talking about.

All you need to know about Mr. Slater's English class is summed up with one visual. He stands at the board, back to the class, and twitches his butt muscles.

One cheek. The other cheek.

Back and forth.

Left and right.

Right and left.

The entire lecture, the entire fifty-eight minutes, is him talking and twitching and all of us trying not to watch the grotesque display. It's a bit like the cobra and the mongoose, although not really, because he doesn't ever turn around to see if we're hypnotized or not.

And, as far as I know, he's never bitten a student. Though if he turned up on *Dateline*, I wouldn't be one of the people saying, "Oh, we had no idea. He was always so nice and quiet."

The other thing is, we're working on our term papers. (Quarter papers to be accurate, but Mr. Slater doesn't care about accurate.) We're supposed to compare and contrast Edgar Allan Poe and Ernest Hemingway.

I title my paper "The Crackhead and the Suicidal Alkie." Mr. Slater looks over my shoulder, wheezes through his chin-length nose hair and tells me, "That won't do."

No other explanation.

How's that for crappy teaching? Isn't he supposed to be supportive and foster my young mind?

Hello? Show of hands—how many of us in the world are forced to compare old dead guys who obviously tried to work their issues out on the page, and later killed themselves, or overdosed, instead of actually getting therapy? The answer is simple: all high school students. Everywhere.

I mean, if the dead guys couldn't understand what they wrote, why the heck do the rest of us have to try to make sense of it? Have you ever had a conversation with a stoner that was deep and intellectual?

The script goes like this:

Normal nondrugging Brain: 'Scuse me.

(Continue to stand there, and wait for Zoner to move out of the way to the locker room door. Make obvious signals about ticking off seconds until the tardy bell rings.)

(With a glazed slow-mo stare, Zoner notices you standing there. He holds out a self-rolled cig like it's manna. Exaggerated facial expression of devotion.)

Zoner: You want some?

Brain (speaking softly and slowly, as if being stalked by a wild animal): Could you just move? Away from the door?

Zoner (Looks around. Surprise evident on face.): This door?

Brain (Smile, nod. Repeat. Careful to move at the pace of Elmer's glue.): That's the one.

Zoner (said with excitement): Hey, Billy, did you know there's a door there?

Billy: No! (*After shouting, Billy dissolves into a pool of unshowered hilarity.*)

Zoner (breaking into gales of laughter, barely can be understood): Yeah, man.

Now, why in a hundred years, or even fifty, would I ask future generations to decipher the greatness of the door? I mean, really—let's look at Poe here. Doors, windows, floorboards. Ticking clocks, for heaven's sake.

Hemingway just tried to get gored at every turn. Not hard to do when falling down drunk. But he also fished, so drowning was a theme for him too.

I really am on the right track. Mr. Slater, being a white man of dubious character, wouldn't understand that. *Breathe, Gert. Breathe.*

Tangent: sorry.

Lucas sits one row, one desk up.

He has the most adorable curl of dark chocolate on the back of his neck. Sometimes it hides under his shirt collar, or disappears for a few weeks when his mother insists he get his hair cut, but it's like Punxsutawney Phil and always reappears.

7

It's a cold autumn, so right now he basically wears jeans, dark denim or slightly worn, hiking boots, hoodies in black or gray and a T-shirt from one of the million soccer camps he's been to. He usually has a soccer ball between his feet that he rolls back and forth, in the butt-clenching tempo set by Mr. Slater.

(I'm fairly certain this is a subconscious coincidence and he's not into Mr. Slater's butt or anything. Like I said, mongoose-cobra. It's all hypnotic.)

Lucas occasionally smiles at me. Like yesterday when we did this ridiculous alliteration with our names. I'm Gert. Gertrude Doyle Garibaldi, to be all official.

Yeah, nice to meet you, too.

My parents were shocked by my arrival, not like they didn't have nine months to get used to the idea. They don't appreciate when I point this out. It's not as if the stork dropped me off. But they missed the memo on gestation. See, my mom was forty-five when she found out she was pregnant, and my dad sixty.

My brother, Mike, graduated from college that spring. I guess I can see why they were surprised.

In momentary astonishment that's lasted sixteen years and counting, they had a complete loss of sense when they named me. Either that, or they'd forgotten what it was like to be a kid, and picked the ugliest name on the planet just to see what kinds of hell a name can conjure.

They were too far removed from kidland, even from thirtiesville, to realize that Heather or Jessica or Amanda would have been much better choices.

But hello? *Gertrude?* The shock excuse only goes so far to get them off the hook. The worst part is, it's not even a family name. There's no reason at all they had to name me Gertrude.

I'm breathing. In. Out.

Tangent: sorry.

Anyway, yesterday Mr. Slater decides we have to make up sentences with our name and a minimum of three other words. We can use our own name for the first five sentences, then switch to anyone else's in the class.

Want to guess whose name is the most popular for this assignment?

Gigantic Gert gallops gratefully.

Gremlins gobble Gert's gonads. (Of course, we have to have a sex reference.)

Then Lucas raises his hand and says, "Gorgeous

Gert gambles." He tosses a smile over his shoulder at me.

A perfect moment until Mr. Slater ruins it and says, "Fascinating, but not enough words, Mr. Miers. Who wants to finish it?"

Then I'm back to gambling garbanzo beans and gizzards.

Still, it's a brief, beautiful moment.

Saturday and PSAT day. Which stands for Public Stress and Terror.

It's not really a test of what you know. It's more a test of whether you're capable of disarming a bomb at gunpoint.

I show up at a neighboring school's campus, just one of many faceless hopefuls flipping through prep books and flash cards like cramming the last twenty minutes before the test is enough to bump up the score. Me, if I tried studying right before the test, I would mix up my name and answer "c" for confused on everything.

So we stand in the cold, not looking at each other,

hoping that everyone besides ourself is below average rather than above average. It's this line of averageness.

The instructors lead us into the cafeteria in single file, like animals at a slaughterhouse. They hand us pencils silently, no talking at all. Not even the adults are speaking. A guy in a navy blazer and navy cords takes our bags (he's got to be Secret Service), including all the prep books and flash cards. Time's up, kiddies, now you must rely solely on your brain.

I'm fairly certain there are video cameras hidden around the room, and if you appear too calm and collected, guys in navy blue suits and earpieces come in and whisk you away to a special school. There's a red light blinking in the globe dangling above my head.

The first true challenge of the morning: Where to sit? By the window? Facing it or with my back toward it? Next to the Goth Girl or the Ennui-Art Kid? I dismiss a table of jocks; they'd suck the smarts right out of me.

Honestly, who wants to fill in bubbles with a number two pencil to answer questions no one really needs to know the answers to?

Do they have you balance a checkbook?

Change the car oil?

Defend yourself against frosh hazing?

Nope, they care about synonyms and geometry and whether or not you follow the toad when they swap him out for the turtle in the story.

And, if it's really supposed to measure our knowledge, why do we get to take practice tests?

I'm antsy. I squirm in my seat, wondering if I can move quickly to another table before the test starts. I can't make up my mind. A normal-looking girl plunks down across from me and I open my mouth to say hello, but no sound comes out when she glares at me. No talking, in the body language way of speaking, is a little rude.

An overpaid drone is passing out the booklets.

Why do we get to take the SAT as many times as we want? Though you really can't take it more than three times, according to Dan Smith in PE. He's been in high school an extra year because he can't quite pass all his requirements. Of course, the sleeping during classes, working to support his three kids and time he's away "visiting relatives" (he's really in prison on those sabbaticals, though I have no idea if he has family members there or not, so he might not be lying, technically) can't help things. Anyway, he's not what I'd call a reliable source of info.

And yes, I'm taking the PSAT as a sophomore, but I'm *so* not the only one in America getting a practice shot at it. It's pretty standard if you think you're going to college, or your guidance counselor thinks you're going to college, or your parents think you're going to college and convince the guidance counselor there's a chance you're going to college. Then you take it early just to see.

My mother started the day making me eat a mixing bowl of oatmeal cement, two rubber eggs, burnt toast, a mealy apple and almost-bad milk. All I can think about is vomiting. Or trying not to. Or wishing I would so I'd feel better.

Pepto, Pepto, where art thou, lovely Pepto?

I sit at my desk and stare at all the bubbles waiting to be filled in like gasping mouths. Like dying goldfish in the algae pond of life.

Name. Birth date. Social Security number. Even these do not come automatically to mind this morning.

And I hear my heart, no kidding, hammer in time

to the damn ticking clock. With every heartbeat, I sit there one step closer to having no future.

The rebel in me wants to fill in all the circles in a pretty smiley-face pattern and not care.

Sadly, I'm not brave enough to laugh it off.

I'm actually trying to do well. What if I'm not as smart as I think I am? What if I'm in the lowest percentile of stupid?

Blub-blub. Blub-blub. That's my heart trying to get out and run away screaming. My palms are sweaty. I have an insane itch in my left nostril.

The loudspeaker crackles to life. There's a bit of heavy breathing. "You may begin." I think God just started our PSAT, because nowhere in the room is there a microphone. A countdown clock flashes and starts ticking back the seconds. It's like a freaky sporting event with no cheerleaders.

We'll see how my score turns out. About the time I'll forget the terror of taking the test, the score sheet will show up to remind me. Like a dead horse. Or a really bad zit.

"Gert, sweetheart, can I come in?" Mom knocks on the door like I'm a sleeping dragon.

Roar. "Sure." It's not like I'm trying to work or anything important. Hemingway can wait.

"How are you?" Mom perches on the edge of my bed. She asks this with emphasis on the "are." She makes "are" sound like it should come with a decoder ring and instruction manual. Like she's not sure what to say.

"Fine." I would grunt, but I think that'd startle her. She's a very sensitive soul.

"Good. That's good." Her gaze wanders around the room like it's Queen Nefertiti's undiscovered tomb.

That's me—the archaeological find of the century. I'm digging that. "What's up?" I ask, hoping to snap her back to the present. Mom's eyes are getting a little glazed and wild.

"Oh. Yes." She shakes it off and twitters. I am so glad I didn't inherit the twitter. "I brought you a little welcome back to school present."

She hands me a book wrapped in the comics section of Sunday's paper. It's impossible to fake that I don't know a book when I'm handed a book. Why wrap books? (Uh, obscure the title, that'll make it a surprise.)

"Thanks." I hold the book, hoping she won't make me open it in front of her.

"Go on." She shoos me with her hands.

"Okay." I slowly unstick the tape and drag the book out of the paper. I'm mentally practicing my make-Mom-happy smiley face and rehearsing my reaction because I really can't be too genuine around here.

The back is pink. It has a little gold-like lock. I have a moment of panic. There's a collective teen gene that tells me this is the diary that every girl gets when she's eight. I'm not eight.

I turn it over, forcing my eyebrows and lips into position onstage. "Wow." Wow is right. Yep. Wow.

"Do you like it? I remember my first diary when I was your age, and I really appreciated having a safe place"—she taps the lock with her index finger—"where I could record my feelings. Because we know you have feelings, Gertrude. And your dad and I want you to have an outlet that's healthy and safe."

Does she think my feelings are going to start World War III? I'm not that emotional. I'm more a third-world Latin American coup than a nuclear standoff.

"And I just really thought this one was perfect for you."

Perfect? Fake gold script declaring *My First Diary*? And it has a sheep on it. A deformed Quasimodo meets a leper love child kind of sheep. I can't hold it back. I really try, I do. "Is that a sheep?" I squint at the cover. I just broke the too-honest rule.

"Gert, that's a unicorn." Mom laughs like I'm the funniest girly ever.

"Really?" I'd say a sheep with overlarge scapulas and a nasty zit in the middle of its forehead. Frankly, I can't think of a better place to confide my deepest darkest secrets.

"It's a unicorn." She's starting to figure out I'm not kidding. She takes the diary from me in an overly aggressive manner and stares at the cover. "Yes, it's a very cute unicorn." She hands it back and taps my cheek. "My little girl is growing up."

"Yep." What else is there to say? *Nice of you to notice?*

"Okay then. I'll leave you and your book alone. Is that for English?"

I glance at *The Sun Also Rises* propped against my pillows. Like I'd read that for fun. "Yep."

"Interesting." She walks to the door.

I always seem to disappoint her and here again I

can feel it in the air. I don't know what she wants from me. I don't know how to give it. "Mom."

She turns with her hand on the doorknob.

"Thanks. For the diary, I mean." I clear my throat.

"You're welcome." She lightly shuts the door.

I look at the diary. "You have got to be kidding." It's a sheep. A sheep that will live in the complete darkness and chaos that is the floor of my closet.

rant #1
on high school

I wonder if the aliens walking among us feel as out of step as I do. There's all this crumping and stepping and sidewinding, and I'm the damn fox-trot. I don't even know what the fox-trot is, but I'm it. In the flesh.

I mean, here's the deal; this is a completely foreign culture. Why do some people have the high school handbook downloaded before birth and others of us are just supposed to muddle through as best we can? How are the chosen people chosen? And how do I get me on that list?

Like we're in a controlled experiment and we're the variables.

"Hey, Scientist Man, look at that girl over there hanging out by the water bottles. Doesn't she look like she'd rather be mucking out stalls on a wildebeest farm than trying to find something to say to Control Group Number One?"

Or "Dude, PhD Man, let's give that guy braces, put zits on his zits and suggest that his father's walkman that plays cassette tapes is on par with listening to an iPod."

Or better yet, the aliens are messing with our minds. The whole UFO thing is set up to throw the humanoid government off track—when, in fact, the aliens are infiltrating the nation's high schools thinly disguised as Pops and Things. Area 51 sounds suspiciously like the science building on campus.

It just can't be like this. I won't accept that for the next three years my life will feel as if I've stepped into someone else's skin and, at any minute, I'll be found out as a fraud. I'm not sure what I really am, but I feel fraudish. Hugely fraudish.

Any minute now, there will be a loud ding and my time will be up.

Any. Minute. Now.

two

Driver's education. Is there anything else I need to say? I could stop there and we'd all have the same mental picture.

We have it before school. *BEFORE SCHOOL*.

Scientists in Denmark have pretty much figured out that teenagers have no brain activity before, like, noon. So why is it we have driver's ed at six-thirty a.m., then adults rail about teens not knowing how to drive? I don't get it.

Of course we don't know how to drive—you're teaching us when we're still asleep.

Joey, Jennifer, Jacob and Jessye all trudge in with me and slide into their chairs. None of us open both eyes. One designated eyeball is exposed to minimal light so we don't run into each other, or walls. Otherwise, the rest of us is asleep.

Driver's ed's in the shop classroom. We don't even rate a real classroom.

And hello? Not having the best and the brightest teach us how to drive either. I'll get to Mr. Fritz in a moment, but let's start with the standard rules of the road if you're a teen driver in this state. Some call them laws, but laws are like Newton and gravity—you have to follow them or there are consequences. These are just rules. No consequences.

Number one: No passengers until you're eighteen unless they're a relative or a legal adult. Has anyone stood outside the student parking lot when last bell rings? We're talking six to eight kids crammed into a Geo Metro. No families are that big.

The cops could sit and make their Christmas bonuses in front of the gate. Line them up and haul them off. It would definitely make the roads safer to get rid of a few of the seniors. As it is, I have never seen a police person anywhere near the campus unless they're giving a presentation about the perils of drug use.

Number two: seat belts. Again with the weird parenting and adultishness.

Here's the deal: seat belts are mandatory in this state. Maybe everywhere except Mars. But fathers are hauling dead cars (without seat belts) out of the junk heap and refurbishing them as good old father-son projects.

They're souping up Cadillacs and Monte Carlos and Marlon Brandos that haven't seen the open road since the first chapter of the U.S. history textbook.

So while they may have engines, they don't have upholstery, let alone seat belts.

Then eight kids cram in and we're back to the first stupid rule that isn't enforced. Corey and his girlfriend, Elaine, are this bettor's sure thing for a yearbook dedication after their vehicular stupidity between now and graduation.

How do adults manage to feed themselves?

Here comes Mr. Fritz shuffling in. If we have to be here by six-thirty, why does he come at six-forty? He's the re-retired football coach from, like, 1960. He uses a walker and has a tank of oxygen on a wheelie cart behind him. His idea of multimedia presentations is filmstrips.

Filmstrips. Not videos. Not media clips. Filmstrips.

One. Frame. At. A. Time.

Oh goody, today is a filmstrip.

"You there. Turn out the lights." Mr. Fritz points at Camille. He has the wheeze of a smoker slowly dying of asphyxiation.

About three days a week, he turns the lights out so we can see the filmstrips. *Hello?* Haven't we already established our eyes are open but there's nothing happening in the Jell-O at this hour?

"Today we're going to view the crash test done by the Department of Motor Vehicles using dummies not wearing their seat belts," Mr. Fritz says.

The dummies are lounging in cars twice our age.

"Pay close attention to the impact on the neck and head," he continues.

Has anyone heard of air bags? I think maybe cars have them now. I tune out Mr. Fritz and his one-frame-at-a-time view of driving. Walking is faster than learning to drive in this class. I mean, who needs a license?

Corey yawns.

I flip open a notebook like I'm taking notes, but really I'm going to make a list of all the reasons Lucas and I should be together. I'm not numbering the list because each reason is as valuable as the others. We are all equal in love.

Ruth yawns.

We are soul mates because he moved here at the perfect time to be my first and only love.

He isn't too fussy about his looks and doesn't seem to notice how incredibly yummy he is.

Blane yawns.

Lucas is in my English class.

My best friend likes his twin.

Cathy the coffee girl snorts like a tapir in the Amazon.

He drinks from the water fountain rather than carrying around an expensive plastic water bottle, which shows his sensitivity and environmental savvy.

Jessye yawns at the same time as Jessica.

His eyes tell me he'd understand me. Really get me.

He has a fantastic smile and he doesn't laugh like a Thingy-Buffoon.

It's a yawning epidemic. I cave. I can't fight the peer pressure and instead close my eyes to spend quality time visualizing our first date.

For God's sake, let's get behind a wheel. We'll learn about car wrecks soon enough.

I am going to hurl all over Ms. Whoptommy's sensible, ugly navy blue shoes. I mean, horrendously go-barefoot-instead ugly.

Who designed them? Jimmy "Ew"?

I was trying to do a good thing. Trying to be responsible and mature—and please hit me in the head the next time I have the urge. Humiliation, anyone? There's an Internet special with my name. For a great low price you get a gynormous helping of humiliation.

Here's the skinny. I sent Ms. Whoptommy an informational, nonjudgmental e-mail proposing that Jenny downloaded her paper from www.theultimatetermpaper .com. I saw her go to the Web site, pick the paper, attach her little USB cable and download a whole freakin' paper she's calling hers.

I'll be honest. I don't like Jenny Cohen. Everyone knows that. Even Ms. Whoptommy knows Jenny and I would rather be on opposite ends of the world than have to sit next to each other.

Jenny smells.

Jenny has an infected nose piercing.

Jenny smiles like she means it, then spits on you.

Jenny is above all else the soon-to-be captain of the cheerleading squad (next year).

I thought a little heads-up might be appreciated by the powers that be. Okay, perhaps I hoped Jenny might get punished in a seriously unspeakable manner. So what do I get for my trouble? I'm standing here with the entire class glaring at me.

Ms. Whoptommy says, "Jenny, do you have anything you'd like to say in response to this slanderous accusation?"

Jenny says, "Well, if Gert were more tech-savvy, she'd realize I saved my completely-original-nonplagiarized work to my PDA because my printer broke and I needed to print it at school. Really, Gert. I'm hurt. You could have just asked me."

"Are you really buying this—" I break off at the sight of thunderclouds gathered on Ms. Whoptommy's prominent horizon. *She's such a lying skink.* My face has never been quite this on fire. I want to melt into a puddle of goo.

Why is it that adults can't seem to keep up with the

times? How hard is it to request to see the handheld and check files and history? There's a list that'll show it's not Jenny's work.

Duh. Hello?

Jenny just flips her hair and bats her eyes and says in a sweet, don't-turn-your-back-on-me voice that she is "sorry to have caused confusion."

Ms. Whoptommy turns to me. "Why did you be-smirch and slander Jenny?" I stop listening as she goes on and on about knowing all the facts before casting aspersions and Watergate and Clinton smoking or something. "What do you have to say?"

Nothing. There's nothing to say. No one in this class likes me. They are all freaks and morons and, shall we say, popular. "Sorry." It pains me to say it, but it's expected. Clearly.

Has Ms. Whoptommy heard of protecting sources? Is it my fault she's not smart enough to check the story?

She probably still gets up to change the dial on a black-and-white TV. She's preremote.

I will never do the right thing again.

If I had one violent bone in my body, I'd smack Jenny. Really I would, but it'd hurt and I'm not big on pain. I fade into my seat as far down as I can and watch the seconds tick off the old clock on the wall. The bell has never rung as beautifully as it does at the end of this class.

Finally, I walk into calculus; I'm way the youngest person in the class, and who's sitting next to me? Tim.

He appears all innocent and nonchalant. He does casual well, but he's not innocent by any stretch of the imagination. I've heard things from Adam. He's really quite cute, but then, he's an exact physical clone of his brother.

Okay, so here's the deal. Tim likes Adam. Adam likes Tim. But they're scared of moving too quickly and not sure what the general atmosphere toward a same-sex couple will be. It's high school—brutal, people, brutal.

However, some of us just wish they'd go ahead and make out, because the tension is freakin' unbearable and the rest of us would really appreciate a little ebb to that flow.

A girl can only take so much ménage à trap.

Adam is my best friend. We've been friends since we played house and he insisted on decorating it instead of looking at my naked breasts, which were much more interesting. He's smart and funny, and he listens to me rant and hands me Kleenex when I cry. He helps me shop for trendy wardrobe additions, and knows more about beauty regimens than I will ever know.

Clue?

It's not like you'd know he's gay by looking at him. He doesn't have rhinestone sunglasses, a pink boa and tight leather pants. And I know stereotypes are racist and other "ist" things but they had to come from somewhere, right?

Adam played with my Barbies, stitching clothes for them by hand while I built his model planes. I know what you're thinking. My building model planes didn't make me gay, so why does playing with Barbies make him gay? I don't know. But it does.

Adam has always known he's gay, and I wasn't shocked or anything when he told me. I pretty much always knew, probably because we'd kept crush books (notebooks with photos of cute boys) since we were in third grade. He never complained about the hours I spent simpering over Jonathan Taylor Thomas and Johnny Depp. He's just Adam. My Adam. He keeps me steady.

The twins moved here from New York over the summer. Tim and Lucas Miers. Lucas is *the* most deliciousness boy in the world.

In fact, I'd say he's getting manly. Not just boy anymore. There's something hypnotic about manly boys.

Tim is a total jock. He's into every sport. He says he doesn't really like playing, but he's good at everything and keeps his parents happy. Right now he's a receiver on the football team, but I guess he runs track in spring and plays baseball in the summer.

So I have calc with Tim, who is also smart, obviously, and once or twice a week he'll sit next to me during class so we can toss notes. I think I must give off an okay-with-gay vibe that's nonthreatening.

We really have to Dark Age it because if Casperelli caught us with phones or BlackBerries, we'd be totally suspended. So we keep sheets of paper out under our math texts and write questions and answers. Honestly, I can't say I know Tim very well. He's either grilling me about Adam or we're doing weird "would you rather" questions like "Would you rather lick Jack Black's big toe or the green slime that gathers at the shower drains in the locker room?" I'm still not clear on my answer.

The rows are so squashed, it's not like Tim even has to lean over to read and vice versa. Plus, we make like we're doing our work together.

Casperelli doesn't care. He's the track coach and supposedly a poet. Why they have him teaching calc is beyond me.

Tim leans in and writes, "How are things?"

Translation: *Does Adam still adore me?*

"Fine," I scribble.

Translation: *Of course he does, you idiot! Would you please get off your duff and ask the boy on a real date so the rest of us mere hetero sapiens can get back to the thing we call life?*

Tim: "You have plans on Friday night?"

Translation: *Can you show up with Adam somewhere and pretend to be invisible while we have a date so I can pretend I'm not totally into him in case anyone sees us?*

I have to think about it. I don't want to be mean, but if you pay attention to HBO, and who doesn't, "fag hag" is a term that can completely and totally ruin a girl.

Tim isn't out to the general populace. I wouldn't say he hides it, but he doesn't do PDA and he doesn't have the flamboyance that's so difficult for total femme gay guys to hide. He's a jock, and it's easier for him to blend without controversy.

Adam's a little more out because, frankly, if you have any gaydar, he's a big ol' bleep on the screen. He's been shoved around a couple of times and gets called names occasionally. I don't want my best friend beat up; I volunteered early on to be the safety hetero so get-togethers look like group things as opposed to gay dates.

I'm not a saint. After three not-date dates where I watched my gum dissolve in my Diet Coke, I'm getting a little tired of the whole hag scene. It's depressing to watch two otherwise intelligent boy-men smile and giggle and gape at each other.

"Why don't you invite Adam over and rent a movie?"

Translation: *You're a big boy, act like it.*

Tim's face falls. "Parents gone."

Translation: *I don't have the balls.*

I raise my eyebrows. "So?"

Translation: *Grow some.*

"Lucas said he'd be there, so if you came it would be a group thing." Tim writes fast, then looks at me pleadingly. He doesn't know I drool over his brother.

At least I haven't told anyone officially that I get all hot and fluttery when Lucas is around.

Like I would go if I don't want to, just because Lucas is going to be around.

Around. In his house. Maybe in his boxers if I catch him unawares. Or is it unaware?

"What time?" I give in. What can I say? I'm a horny girl with aspirations of action. While I wouldn't have a clue what to do if I actually caught Lucas in his Underoos, it's too deliciousness an opportunity to miss.

I wonder if he's a briefs or boxers kind of guy?

I think he probably has a six-pack from all the sports—

Tangent: sorry.

Back to Tim and Adam. I get that outing yourself to the world can be difficult. I'm not going to stand up in the cafeteria and announce I'm hetero. Not anyone's business, and the Pops would all laugh.

I don't look like Paris Hilton or Hilary Duff, so obviously my sexual preferences are a little moot in high school.

I don't cheer. I don't belong to the school band. I'm

smart. Not only can I spell "syphilis," I can spell "pregnant" and "so not going to happen."

I mean, it's pretty useless if I'm realistic.

But Tim and Adam like each other. I mean, really like each other. What's the big bloomin' deal if they want to date?

Why they think the school photographer is going to pop up like paparazzi and rat them out, I don't know. I think there's a certain paranoia that sets in when you live and breathe and want to be testosterone.

So I guess we have plans Friday night. Whoop, dawg. I can't wait.

rant #2
the players
(a guide to groups)

Things:

Things are those guys who shave daily, forget to wear deodorant but swim in cologne. It's like they slept through the most important part of health and hygiene only to wake up during the optional lessons on appearance.

They always have cars with loud roaring engines.

They always have girlfriends, or they have a posse of freshman girls following them around like a gaggle of Giggles.

There's usually a sport attached to their persona like a leech, but sometimes they go with the bad-boy image and blow smoke in the general direction of organized anything.

They can be any grade level but usually reach full Thingness as upperclassmen, especially seniors.

Giggles:

Giggles always wear the latest and greatest fashions. You name it, they wear it. But they tend to wear it badly. You have to know what I'm talking about. Like one of those flip books where you can pick the top of the person, the bottom and the shoes.

They never actually wear the complete outfit as advertised.

Underclasswomen Giggles tend to cross over into Pops territory as upperclasswomen. Rarely is a senior Giggle spotted except on college campuses, where she simply does an older version of the same routine.

Almost always thin, probably has an eating disorder. Thinks her daddy's credit card is her daddy. Has never been told no in her life and most likely will never be told no until the divorce from her first husband.

I think perhaps the cologne fumes from the Things fry the Giggles' brains.

Pops:

They are known by many names. Popular kids. The in crowd. The Haves. We call them Pops mainly because they're too sweet on the world, have it too easy as far as high school goes, and their little worlds tend to pop upon graduation.

Some are Pops by association—a direct friendship with a complete Pops can pull anyone on the fringes in. Some are Pops by birth, as generations of class photos can attest. Usually they have enough money so they don't have to worry too much about buying vending-machine food, gas or the latest must-have item.

Brains:
   Students like me who see knowledge as power.
We're either born smart or work hard to stay ahead
of the curve. Sometimes called nerds or geeks, but
not always do we fully settle in either distinction.
Brains can be Jocks and on rare occasions Pops,
usually by birth. We're the ones who do the homework, know the answers and get along with teachers better than students. We're the future CEOs,
presidents of Fortune 500s, chairmen, surgeons,
corporate attorneys. Basically, the bosses and paycheck
providers, in ten years, of any aforementioned groups.

Cloud Riders:
   Aka Zoners, Stoners, Druggies, the Sensory
Impaired. Those to whom brain cells aren't important, who imbibe, snort, smoke, shoot, huff, cram,
coax or otherwise ingest foreign substances for a
quick high and a life of addiction.

Wannabes:
   Aka "in training." Can apply to any group but
most often are Things and Pops Wannabes. Often a
younger sibling learning the social mores and cus-
toms, but can also be a transfer student. Saddest
incarnation is Wannabes-Who-Will-Never-Be. These
are the kids who don't know the Joke is on them.

three

We're taking a career aptitude test in fourth period today. Don't these people read *Newsweek? Elle? Glamour? Cosmo?*

We'll all change jobs eight times before we die; notice I didn't say retire because none of us ever will, according to the president, and my father.

"Yes, Ms. Garibaldi?" The Counselor continues passing out the paperwork.

"If a test can tell us what we should choose to do, don't you think we'd stay in the same job our whole adultness?"

"Well, yes."

"There'd be no point in switching. None. And strangely, the first paragraph of this introduction"—

I point toward the test—"says ninety percent of us will change careers more than five times."

"This test is designed to help get you started, and who knows, Ms. Garibaldi, maybe you'll be in the ten percent who never change careers." Guidance counselor extraordinaire, also drama department chair, doesn't appreciate my wisdom. She scowls and huffs behind her reading glasses.

Now, there's a woman who should be changing careers. Isn't she due to flip burgers somewhere? Okay, maybe that's me.

I shrug. It's not like this is a terribly difficult way to spend a half hour. Just pointless.

So it's quiet for, like, ten minutes as people speed through the questions. I don't think half the class actually reads the questions before coloring in random bubbles.

They make everybody take the test, so by the time I'm sitting here waiting for my results, the results from earlier periods are already out. According to the test, Trevor should be a policeman or an FBI agent. Trevor sells every flavor of meth or prescription pills you'd ever need. He could stock Denmark's entire hospital system. Law enforcement. As what? The drug-sniffing dog?

The test said Maria should be in retail sales. Maria weighs about four hundred pounds, doesn't shower, wears the same clothes every day and rumor has it, lives in a car. By choice. Her dad's a vice president at Microsoft or something. They have an estate larger than Rhode Island. But Maria lives in her car in the twelve-car garage. What is she going to sell, shares in a mental-illness resort?

The test points Isaac toward being a zoologist or a veterinarian. Hmm, the closest Isaac gets to animals is the spectacular case of crabs he picked up on the school trip to Europe last spring. I'm passing along this gossipy tidbit as hearsay; I haven't had firsthand experience with Isaac's terrarium or anything.

Then there's me. Yes, let's talk about my score on the questionnaire. I range in the academic-research portion.

I think anyone who actually reads the test probably gets the same result. We need people who read to teach the people who refuse on basic principles.

I mean, really. Is it a stretch to see me in a lab coat, tenured at the University of Nowhere?

Dear God, I hope it's a stretch.

I want adventure.

I want drama.

I want—it's lunchtime.

Lunch is the highly valued free time when we get a daily reminder just how uncool we really are.

We're little sadomasochists running around waiting for the lunch bell. Counting down the second hand on the outdated clocks. Scribbling our names in the margins of our notes until the glorious buzzing. Then, like locusts, or fruit flies, or some creepy-crawly-low-on-the-food-chain kind of thing, we swarm into lines.

Lines for the bathroom don't apply to the Pops. They merely move to the front like gravity doesn't touch them.

Lines for getting to the teeny-weeny lockers located behind broad Thing shoulders.

You don't want to draw attention to yourself, so you stand there quietly while Thing One and Thing Two belch and fart.

Lines for food most people wouldn't feed their dogs. Again, Pops cut.

Lines around the perimeter of tables, hoping to see someone you recognize before anyone realizes you have no place to sit, because today is the Spanish club, or debate, or jazz rehearsal, and only Pops and Things are in the cafeteria.

It's like one of those Vietnam War movies, only there's no visible blood, but most of us will be talking about the wounds years from now in therapy.

Oh, crap.

No.

No.

No.

Damn.

Breathe.

Look casual. Not dead, casual.

Lucas.

The hair.

Those lips.

That gliding stride.

He's almost here.

Run. Run. Run.

"Hi!" I say way too loud.

I sound like one of those yippy dogs.

He tips his head. Dips it. All cool and nonchalant.

Where do guys learn that? Does someone pull them aside in the locker room and instruct them on the head dip?

The I'm-way-too-cool-to-just-ignore-your-yippy-dog-ass-but-my-vocal-cords-don't-speak-your-language head dip. If you're lucky, they even give you a mock salute or finger wave.

I don't know what's more nauseating: the fact that I like a boy-man who does the head dip or that I am a yippy dog.

I bring an apple, a cheese stick, Oreos and water for lunch. My mother always hands me fifty cents for lunch as I walk out the door. That won't buy a bottle of Coke. Thanks, Mom.

Does she not see me put things in the grocery cart that we never eat for dinner? Does she not see me pack my lunch every morning? Well, to be fair, she always sleeps until five minutes before I leave for school.

I find Adam sitting with Spenser, Clarice, Victor and Greg. They grunt as I sit down. I don't know if we really like each other. I mean, we do publicly, but I'm thinking when we graduate from high school, we'll never see each other again.

Clarice has potential if she gives up talking about femme rock all the time and making I-want-you faces at Spenser. She wears scuffed Airwalks, camo pants and T-shirts with random sayings on them. Her hair is thick, black and straight as a pencil, with a bold thatch of bangs at her eyebrows.

The only statement Victor and Greg make with their clothes is whether or not their mommies have done laundry recently. Victor plays Dungeons & Dragons. Greg plays chess.

Spenser is an unashamed nerd who doesn't care that his photo appears in every academic club in the yearbook. He'd really like to add jock to his résumé but at five-five that's not going to happen. He keeps praying for muscles, though.

The thing is, Adam has been friends with this group since kindergarten. And friends with me since only second grade.

In some sick hierarchy of social stratospheres, I have to be nice to them or he gets mad at me. He can make rude comments all he wants to later, but I can't agree too loudly or I get griped at. It's a very difficult position.

Basically, they're cool people. They're not Pops. But then, Brain here, so neither am I. We're on the outside, which can be all we have in common most days. But it's a bonding thing to not fit in. Unless you really don't fit in, and then there's always the bathroom stalls for lunch.

Here's the conversation:

"I hate math. Swear you'll kill me the day before the midterm," Clarice says, not convincingly. She gets Bs only because she refuses to study. Otherwise, I'm sure she'd set the curve.

"No prob. Just don't haunt me," Victor says.

Clarice shrugs. "Don't believe in ghosts. Do you?" She directs this at Spenser. She directs everything at Spenser.

Victor answers, oblivious that he's no longer necessary to the conversation. "Nope."

"I saw one," Spenser offers through a mouthful of French fries.

Clarice leans forward. "Saw one? A ghost?" I think she must have read last month's *Elle* article on enticement. If she flips her hair—yep, she read the article.

Victor guffaws. "That was your dick, asshole." He gets high fives from Greg and Adam.

"No, man. I saw my grandmother wearing this old white thing." Spenser, of course, now feels the need to explain.

"Her skin?" I offer.

"No, never mind." He shakes his head and crams more fries in his mouth.

"I want to know." Almost daily our fifteen minutes of lunch is Clarice trying to get Spenser to talk about . . . anything.

They've had some seriously-should-be-on-*Saturday-Night-Live* exchanges. It would be funny if it wasn't real.

"Nah. Forget it." Spenser stuffs the rest of his burger in his mouth and pushes back from the table.

He doesn't bother with goodbye. He never does. He always runs away when he realizes Clarice is staring at him like he's edible.

So Spenser rushes to the gym and tries to have a seizure by playing basketball after swallowing loads of food. I don't think the food even really makes it to his stomach before he's jumping and running and shooting. I'd say dunking, but he's likelier to be dunked himself by senior Things.

The rest of lunch is Victor eating his daily dosage of Twinkies, Hostess cupcakes and Ruffles chased by Mountain Dew. A very nutritious vending-machine meal.

Clarice just sighs. Pouts. Sighs again. Until she realizes she's being obvious, and then she'll ask me whether I like Avril Lavigne or the Ramones.

We have the same conversation every day.

I'm not kidding.

Clarice: "Gert, you think Avril stole her sound from the Ramones?"

Me: "Nope, she's definitely unique. Though I hear angry femme rock foundation in a couple of the songs."

Clarice: "Oh."

Me, feeling sorry for her: "But I really like the Ramones, too."

"Yeah, me too." Clarice brightens. " 'Strength to Endure' is, like, my favorite song."

Now, here's where it gets dicey. If I act too interested, she'll start singing, *American Idol*–style bad. But if I don't, then I get to look at her puppy-dog pout the last ten minutes of lunch. So I tend to tell Adam I have notes for him from bio and he has to come get them right now.

I pull Adam toward our lockers to tell him about the Friday-night plans.

"You're picking me up at seven."

"I am?" Adam never picks me up.

I'm putting my foot down. "Yes, I am not taking the bus to your date."

"Okay." He sees the wisdom in not arguing. He's had his license two weeks and his parents already bought him a very nice car. I think it makes his parents feel better about the queasy, not-really-okay-having-a-gay-son thing they're dealing with. Not that they've said anything other than "I love you, Adam." But he can tell. His dad doesn't hit him in the arm anymore, leaving bruises as tokens of affection. He's stopped dragging him to the garage to change the oil, or spark plugs, or to play with tools.

Adam kinda misses his dad. I can tell.

"Are we ordering pizza?" I will be fed. And fed well. Especially if Lucas isn't around. If he's around, I'm bound to feel serious nausea and lose five pounds in one evening.

"Sure."

I spell things out. "So bring money."

"Do you think—" Adam stops and clears his throat.

Uh-oh, predate jitters just started. I think I will be ill. "No, it'll be great. Fun. Fine. Perfect." I nod until I'm sure my head is going to pop off and roll across the floor, ricocheting off lockers and legs.

"Really?"

Sweet. He's so sweet when he's nervous.

"Really. It'll be great. And if it sucks, I can always get my period and massively bad cramps, and you'll have to rush me home immediately."

This is pretty much my solution to any awkward moment.

"Good. Okay." He looks away and grimaces. "Gross, I hate girls who do that."

I look over to where Adam is pointing to see a Giggle bending over showing all of us the rhinestones at the top of her purple thong.

"Too much information."

"I don't get girls who do that," he says, shaking his head.

"I can't say I understand guys who wear their jeans below the open fly of their boxers, either." I smile.

"Good point."

The bell rings. Lunch over and it's going so well, too. "I can't be late to health. See you later."

"Seven."

"Seven."

Dear Lord, I know we're not real familiar and everything, but please let Lucas walk around in his boxers, and let Adam hold Tim's hand even for just five minutes. Either that or could you strike me with lightning? Life is a little boring right now. A-WOMEN. I just hate saying A-men. So sexist.

rave #1
to thong goes the glory
("PLS" doesn't spell "please")

Listen up, ladies. You're no longer forced to suffer from PLS. Panty Line Syndrome is a very serious disease affecting the middle-aged and very uncool youths. It can strike either gender but most often hits women and girls. It is contagious and can be passed down from mother to daughter for generations.

However, after a simple self-diagnostic, you too can seek treatment. Symptoms include bulges over the elastic waistband at the waist and on the thighs. Most commonly this disease affects wearers of granny panties, worn too high on the stomach and too low on the leg. If a casual observer can easily make out the elastic through your outer garments, you have PLS. If you can run your hand over your fanny and easily feel your panty line, you have PLS.

There is nothing to be ashamed of, but you must seek treatment immediately. Go to the nearest department or lingerie store and try on a thong. These are not shoes, they are underwear. And though they take some getting used to, they are surprisingly comfortable. They come in a variety of materials and sizes as well as colors. Treatment for PLS can be as unique as you are.

A word of caution, though: There is such a thing as too much thong. Do not wear a thong pulled up to the small of your back if you are wearing lowriders. When you bend over, we can all see your thong. We don't want to see your thong. I counted eight thongs in two class periods yesterday. These are recovering PLS sufferers who feel the need to show everyone they no longer have a panty line. We do not need to know. Please keep your thong in your pants. It's not sexy. It's not cute. It's underwear. To be worn under. You want to accessorize an outfit, get new shoes. Earrings. A nice necklace. Leave the thong on your butt and out of my sight.

For the sake of disclosure, I proudly admit I own a thong. Several, in fact. However, unless you seduce me or paw through my panty drawer, you will not see them. Repeat after me: "Thongs are personal and private." Keep saying that until you believe it. I am thong, hear me roar.

four

Here's the deal. I'm standing pretty much nude, in the middle of my bedroom, because I have nothing to wear.

I have clothes, sure, a closet full of mommy-approved high-waisted slacks and tunic tops. Not the stuff of teenage lust.

Not that I'm really excited about the lowriders that basically defy physics by hanging on the apex of an ass. Or the girls who wear thongs up to their navels so we all know they're wearing thongs.

As if the thong is now the pinnacle of adultness.

Tangent: sorry.

So I'm standing here in utility boy shorts and a cotton bra, color confidential. You can tell a lot about the woman beneath the bra when you know what her color preferences are. If boys only knew there was a cheat sheet as simple as the Victoria's Secret catalog.

I repeat. I have nothing to wear. Nothing.

I settle on a skirt I can roll up on the waist once parental units are waved off. A camisole and pullover sweater. If I desire, I can remove the sweater and have simply-sexy cami. It would help if I had cleavage. Or if I knew what sexy felt like, so I would know if I've achieved it.

I flop onto the middle of my bed, staring up at the ceiling. I hate my comforter. It's old. It's pink. It's got Hello Kitty on it. A big ol' Hello Kitty smack in the middle of the mattress. My mother refuses to let me change it until it's worn out.

Fine.

I wash it twice a week. If she only knew she's killing salmon and polluting the water supply with this asinine mandate, I'm sure she'd cave. But until then, cheap laundry detergent and extra spin cycles have the smallest of holes starting at Kitty's whiskers. I think it's made of high-grade, nuclear-proof cotton, though, because I've been washing it since sixth grade.

I hope before I graduate I'm allowed to upgrade to

black. Or gray. Or something that doesn't have a name or merchandise associated with it. Do you have any idea what it does to a girl's psyche to wake up to pink Hello Kitty every morning since fourth grade? Okay, in fourth and fifth grades I still thought it was cool. Sixth grade was the turning point.

Tangent: sorry.

Did today have to be the bad hair day? Isn't there a quota for bad hair days? Like once you've had twelve in a month, you're immune? Is there no God? No Supreme Being watching over us? Caring about our hair?

Maybe not.

I inherited my father's floppy, nondescript, dirty-looking-no-matter-how-clean-it-is hair. Of course, I'm basing this on photographs. He's bald now. Has been my whole life.

I hope I didn't inherit that. I look really bad in hats.

Hair. I need to do something with the hair. I've never been to Lucas's house. Okay, so it's Tim's house too, and he's the one the indirect invite came from. Let's not quibble. Must have perfect hair.

I put it up.

I let it hang down.

I straighten it.

I mousse it.

I try the hippie twist of Kirsten Dunst fame. I'm obviously not Kirsten Dunst.

Now I look like I have a dead kitty on my head.

6:42.

Roadkill, sexy me.

6:42 and ten seconds.

6:42 and thirty seconds.

I rummage around for shoes. Flats. Sandals. Flipflops. Sneakers from gym class last year.

Oo, the combat boots Adam and I found at the flea market last summer. I like to imagine they've been to war and survived.

6:47.

I reapply mascara. I want those big, thick, manic lashes. It really doesn't matter how many times I reapply; I never get lashes like that—mine are puny.

Lip. Gloss. Check. My lips look pouty and kissable, and I wonder if Lucas will try to back me into a closet and have his way with me.

Maybe I can back him into a closet? Is that too forward?

Does being forward ever work? I mean, take Clarice. She's so forward, she pretty much has to walk backward to speak to Spense. It's not working so well for her.

6:54.

No, I'll be demure. I'll be Jane Austen and Mandy Moore.

6:55.

God, I hope this goes well. For Adam. But especially for me. I need a kiss.

I've never had one, and life is fairly abysmal. A kiss has to be at least an improvement. Right?

It can't make things worse.

My pink fuzzy phone rings. I've tried washing it, but aside from a gurgle when it rings, sadly it survived.

It's Adam. Caller ID, blessings upon you.

I don't bother with nice. I'm not feeling nice. I don't have nice hair. Plus, it's not like I'm wanted this evening for me—nope, I'm the hetero chaperone for two very uptight boys. "Where are you?" I snap.

"Outside your house. You know if I come in your parents will corner me with an inquisition."

Adam's right. My parents pretty much decided he had nefarious inclinations around the time we hit puberty. Of course, trying to explain I'm not his type doesn't work. They never believe me. And Adam won't let me tell them he's gay because he's afraid they'll freak out.

I keep trying to explain that gay in their vocabulary means happy—they'll be fine with it. I swear I'd have to have diagrams and flowcharts to convince them he's anything other than really cheery. Adam doesn't buy it.

"On my way." I slam down the phone. Not cuz I'm mad, but because I'm hoping the ear thingy will break if I keep slamming it. My brother gave me that phone. It was really nice of him when I was ten. Now, I curse the girlfriend who thought shopping for his little sister was cute.

I grab my bag, and a book—because we all know there's a possibility I'll be ditched on the back porch if Adam and Tim decide to make out. Makeup blotting papers for shiny moments. They don't work. I bought them in a fit of girliness. I think I channeled a Giggle. A PowerBar, Cookies & Cream, in case we get lost in the urban jungle and are wandering for days looking for sustenance.

Here we go.

I'm going to try saying the affirmation in this month's *Cosmo:* "I am a confident, beautiful young woman who can do anything she sets her mind to."

Saying "I am a confident, beautiful, my butt couldn't be more bubbly woman" just ruins the affirming.

Is there anything in the world more awkward than going to "his" house for the first time? I don't know what I expect. The two-story brown split-level we park in front of is not it.

"This is it?" I think I expect angels on clouds, strumming banjos. Maybe gates, or a butler, or something. It's plain. It's just a house. Kind of an ugly house.

"That's the address Tim stuck in my locker," Adam says.

The unspoken question: Is Tim setting us up or being sincere? I error on sincere.

"This is it then." We both sit there. I can hear Adam swallow.

"We should go in," I say. I am yards away from where Lucas sleeps and wakes.

"Yep." Neither of us moves.

"Anyone else coming?"

"Don't know," he answers.

"Looks pretty empty. Are we early?"

"Should we drive around the block a couple more times?" Adam reaches for the ignition.

I consider, but if anyone notices, then we'd be all stalkery and end up on *Cops*. "Maybe."

Adam hesitates. "Risky if he's looking out the window."

"True." No going around the block. Again. That would make, like, ten trips in a big square.

"Chew." Adam pulls out Winterfresh gum and pops a piece in his mouth. I grab one too. We speed-chew. Breath-freshening purposes.

"Breath?" I spit my gum out into a Kleenex and motion for him to do the same.

He exhales into his palms. "Check."

"Ready?"

The keys get stuck in the ignition. Adam yanks on them.

"Lights." He forgot to turn off his lights. Last thing we need is to get stranded here. Unless Lucas is wearing nothing but a smile and . . . so not going to happen.

We step out and start up the walkway. I squeeze Adam's hand. This is a big step for him, going from meeting in public as a group to going to Tim's house. I'm just here to make sure no one goes into apoplectic shock and dies before the ambulance arrives. I'm the 911 girl.

Tim waits until we ring the bell. Like he wasn't pacing on the other side of the door watching us walk up. Puh-lease. He opens the door. "Hi." Did someone shower and cologne? *Oh, yes, he did.*

"Hi." Adam smiles back at Tim. I've never seen that smile from Adam. I guess he has a special one for these occasions. I nod. They don't notice.

I trail in behind the boys. Talk about awkward, the house is as silent as the bathroom when Dad's in there on Sunday mornings.

And I'm as invisible as Orlando Bloom at a national lesbian convention.

There's something glaringly wrong with this situation. There's no Lucas.

"Want a soda?" Tim heads toward the kitchen nook.

It's a big house, with a huge front room. All the furniture is laid out so the rooms seem separate, but they're not.

Tim's mother is obviously a Martha Stewart devotee. I have never seen so many badly made ribbon flowers and fake tree sculptures in my life. AstroTurf was not invented to be forced into bunny shapes.

There are even bows on the bottoms of the curtains.

Adam follows Tim. I have no idea what's going on in the kitchen. Although, I hear voices, so sadly I don't think it's very interesting.

I poke around. I sniff. Household cleaner. Cologne. Two kinds of cologne, I think, but no Lucas smell.

I flip over a couple of pillows, wondering if Lucas is in another part of the house. I don't hear anything but Adam's nervous laughter.

No soccer balls. No sweat. No freakin' Lucas.

Tim and Adam walk back toward me like they've just remembered I'm there. Gee, thanks. They're staring at me like they're hoping I'll *poof*, disappear.

I'm not the one who invited herself here, boys. I didn't want to come, remember? This wasn't my idea. I glare at Adam, forcing my thoughts into his brain. He doesn't even look sorry. He just has a dopey grin on his face.

Great. Now I'm just a bitch.

"Let's go down to the basement."

"Basement?" My ears perk up. This could be good. Lucas wants to play it cool. He doesn't know we're destined to date. So he doesn't come to the door to greet my arrival—okay, I can live with that. He'll learn. I'll train him.

"Yeah, we keep the big-screen and PlayStation down there. Mom's not big on the noise factor." Tim leads the way.

And yet she's fine with her sons having friends over when she's away. Odd, but cool.

"Cool." Adam follows, winking at me.

Oh, Holy-Mother-of-Twitching, Adam winked at me.

I am going to hurl.

I clear my throat. Are we going to the basement or the dungeon? There's a steep flight of stairs that really shouldn't be used unless we're in a horror flick.

I feel sweat trickle down my back. Crap. I'm hot.

I should take off my sweater before I stink.

I don't feel sexy. I don't want to take off the sweater.

I'm going to have to take off the sweater or I'm going to be so damp, Lucas will rush me to the hospital thinking I have Ebola.

"Your whole family out?" I try for subtlety.

"Yeah." Tim couldn't be less forthcoming. He sits on the floor and settles down against the sofa.

I perch on the edge of a chair. And look at Adam. I haven't told him I'm in love with Lucas. I think my lust is obvious. Do I ask and risk tipping my hand or do I stay mute? I'm willing Adam to read my mind.

Adam kinda stands there. Oblivious.

"I rented three new releases because I didn't know what you'd like. Call pizza in?" Tim says.

I miss the next sentence. Aren't twins supposedly inseparable? I thought they can't get enough of each other's company because of all those years in the womb together.

"Gerts? Pizza?" Adam hands me the menu and points to the special. "You cool with this?"

I'd be cooler if someone pointed the way to Lucas. "Sure." Again I glare at Adam. He ignores me.

Tim punches in the number on his cell. I wonder if Lucas has a cell. And how do I get the number? Not like I'd ever actually call it, but to have it would be nice.

Adam leans down. "Isn't he great?"

I nod. Try to look animated and supportive. "Where's Lucas?"

Shocked, Adam looks around like he hadn't noticed anything missing. "Lucas?"

"You know. Brother to Greatness over there? The guy who was supposed to be here?"

"Oh. He's not, is he?"

You're just now noticing? "No, he's not. In fact, if I didn't know he lived here, I'd swear he'd moved to Tibet."

I really don't feel very good. All that preouting adrenaline has bottomed out and now I just feel ill. Nauseous. Tired. Like I would have had a much better evening watching reruns of *This Old House* with my dad.

Tim hangs up. "It'll take about thirty minutes. It's a Friday night. Want to play Bond till it gets here, or start a flick?" *Oh, joy! A video-game massacre. Delightful.*

Adam leaps to attention, Lucas forgotten. Crap, now *I* have to bring him up.

"Where's your brother?" I do not sound nearly unconcerned enough. I feel neurotic.

"He'll be here. He has practice." Tim doesn't seem to notice my anxiety and goes back to killing animated bad guys who look suspiciously like pro wrestlers.

"Soccer?" His soccer practice would have been over at five. Maybe 5:30. It's now 7:50. Does Tim think I won't notice?

"Yeah, then he had some study group." Tim doesn't take his eyes off the screen.

It sounds suspiciously like Tim didn't really sure up the evening with Lucas. Like he didn't explicitly tell his brother to be here. Why would he? Tim and Adam wouldn't want another guy around—especially a relative. *I'm an idiot. Truly a moron.*

I drag off my sweater. Sexy I'm not, but hot I am, and since it is rapidly becoming apparent that I am the Friday-night fag hag, I want to at least be comfortable.

I rummage in my bag for a rubber band and throw my hair up on my head. Forget roadkill—my lip gloss is gone from serious overlicking of the lips. My nose is, I'm sure, shiny. If I cross my eyes just so, I can see a definite glare.

Well, at least Tim and Adam seem to be having a good time. It's like watching my younger cousin wear my hand-me-downs. Cute, but vaguely sad, too.

I read a whole freakin' chapter of *A Tale of Two Cities*. I don't need to explain how long the chapters are, either.

A Tale of Two Butt Cheeks will be what I title my life story. Because if tonight is any indication, I am a total ass. A moron. A full moon of idiocy.

Fifteen minutes. Half an hour passes at microbial speed.

There is stomping on the steps above my head. Lucas?

Tim hears it too. "Must be Lucas."

Then I hear the giggle. Lucas does not giggle.

There is clomping on the stairs and I can't resist tugging my sweater back on. I don't have time to take my hair down. I'm not ready for Lucas to show up.

There are two sets of feet.

Lucas's, and strappy heels.

He's brought a girl. Sue Seymour. A senior.

No, this is not happening to me. I want to scream. I want to hurl. I want to get out of here.

"Pizza guy pulled up as we got here." Lucas tosses soda cans at Tim, Adam and me. He throws me a Diet Coke. Diet Coke? Does he mean something by that? Do I look fat?

"You guys know Sue," Lucas says. Sue smiles. Shyish. Arrogantish, too.

I lift my hand but can't bring words to my tongue. When did he start seeing her? Are they serious? Is he trying to make me jealous?

And Sue Seymour? She's nice. She has a disabled brother who she takes care of because her mother is divorced and works two jobs.

Lucas brought another girl on our date and he didn't even have the decency to bring one I could hate. I want to hate her, but she's totally unhateable.

Must wipe crushed look off face. I am calm. I am collected. I am the two cheeks of a very large butt.

Adam hands me a plate with two slices of pepperoni. My acting skills must not be Academy level because he says all sweet, "I'll make it up to you."

"No, you won't." I bite into the pizza and smile at Sue, who sits down in the chair next to me. We are girls in a guys' world.

Somehow united, but not friends.

Diet Coke, my ass.

rant #3
parentals and extensions

My parents are so completely and utterly in their own little world, I'm screaming on the inside and smothering my face with a pillow. I know no one can choose their families, but come on. Why didn't their old and shriveled reproductive organs fail when it came time to make me? What in Darwin's hell is the point of saddling me with such ancient relics?

Mike got to play T-ball and Little League. Mike got to go on parent-child camping trips and outings with the Boy Scouts. The parentals taught Mike to drive in the family car. His birthday was always a huge party with tons of people. I've seen the photos, there's evidence. But me? I'm an afterthought.

I have parents who are tired. I mean, truly tired. There are no more tired people in the entire world. You'd think if they got some decent sleep they'd be fine, but no. They go to bed at odd hours and get up to wander in the wee hours and act like they're doing me a favor inquiring about my day.

I feed myself. I do my own laundry. I arrange for my own transportation. I ground my own butt if I get a bad grade. I've never misbehaved in my life because they couldn't keep up if they wanted to.

What's with that? I want parentals who are normal ages. I want a brother who isn't so old his teachers have retired. I never hear "Oh, you're Michael Garibaldi's little sister." Nope, his teachers are dead by the time I show up.

I have to beg for anything technologically in this century. Our answering machine uses a tape instead of a digital chip. We have a VCR. Heaven forbid we have cell phones. I can't have a computer that's from this millennium because we have to wear out the one we have before we can replace it. The processor is so old, it's quicker to hand-calligraphy assignments rather than type them. And forget high-speed anything; nope, we're dial-up. DIAL-UP! Yep, that sums it up. My family is dial-up.

five

This has to be the single worst night ever. At least of this month, maybe this decade.

And the worst part? I can't leave, because Adam drove and he is ridiculously cute with Tim. I seriously have to keep eating pizza to keep from falling into a forced diabetic coma. Plus, if I try to leave, Adam will get all freaked I'm not being supportive.

Stay, and be miserable. Leave, and piss off best friend. I don't want to be supportive. My stomach hurts. Lucas is so delicious and he keeps smiling at Sue. I am the invisible one.

Here's the deal with Adam and Tim. They're not touching. Nope, couldn't possibly hold hands or anything overt. But let me tell you, the atoms and neutrons slamming into the air around them are seriously nuclear.

I wonder if Lucas knows his brother is gay. There's no way he doesn't know. How could a twin even remotely keep that a secret—can't they read each other's minds? I should ask Adam if Lucas knows. Because if Lucas doesn't know, then maybe he thinks I'm the potential girlfriend for his brother, so he brought Sue to even things up and make it less awkward. Maybe Lucas is trying to be thoughtful and considerate dating Sue in front of me.

I'm neurotic and full of crap. He has to know.

"Those are great boots." Sue points at my combat boots.

"Thanks. Like your sandals." *Aren't your perfectly French-manicured toes cold? It's chilly.*

My lack of shoe trivia is really quite pathetic. It's appalling I haven't been kicked out of the sisterhood of women. Maybe I just need to move to Namibia or Thailand. A place where shoes are optional, or better yet, weird. The women probably critique each other's toes then.

I have ugly toes.

Bad idea.

"I'm hoping to get into State for the fall semester next year." Sue obviously feels the need to chat with me. It must be a boob thing. We have them, therefore we're cohesive.

"Good luck. I hear it's a good school," I say without a hint of malice in my voice. First of all, everyone gets into State. There has never in the history of the college application process been a rejection from there. Even the Cloud Riders, kids so stoned they seem to float through life, get into State. I'm having a hard time not slapping her aware of this fact.

But she's so nice.

So dense.

The boys have turned on a movie I've already seen and didn't like the first time.

Next we'll watch a movie I haven't seen. And never wanted to see. Not even in the guise of watching a movie as an excuse to make out.

I hear that's potentially what can happen.

How would I know?

Sue and Lucas disappear upstairs. He never looks at me. Not once. I don't know where they're going, but I have a very good idea what they are doing.

I button my sweater and long for my bedroom and funky tunes I can crank and sing along with.

Thank God for strict parents, and curfews; we finally have to leave.

The next time I offer to do a good deed, remind me to try out for a girl band instead or be on a reality show as the fat, sincere, ugly girl. The FSUG.

Or maybe throw myself in front of the Route Four school bus. The one with the legally blind bus driver who sued to keep her job.

Or take a trip to Paris and free-fall from the Eiffel Tower. Without a parachute. It'll be less painful than doing the good deed.

Adam hasn't stopped gushing since we got in the car. "That was amazing. He's so funny. And kind. Really, really kind."

"Don't forget cute." I mean, he is Lucas's twin. That we can agree on.

Adam glares at me while he should be watching the oncoming traffic. I guess I'm not faking it very well; I think he's picked up on my disgust and frustration with teenagehood.

At the very least, Lucas could have tried to feel me

up or something. I never got a chance to decide whether or not to let him.

I was so hoping.

Saturday morning is sacred time. The only time in the whole weekend when the hourglass of life seems to stop moving. The time to catch up on sleep ruthlessly stolen by society during the rest of the week.

My parents have forgotten the sacredness of this precious time.

Of course, unless I remind them before bed on Friday, my father is out in the yard mowing the lawn, or trimming the grass edges, or raking the leaves at the crack of dawn. Anything that makes noise under my bedroom window.

Wouldn't you know, my parents had to slog to school barefoot in the snow and help haul in the crops so they didn't starve during the winter? Sleeping in on Saturday morning is an alien concept.

It's only eight.

It's useless.

I'm getting up.

Soon.

My parents neatly stack the week's mail outside my bedroom door. It's full of applications and college brochures. I don't order any.

I don't have to.

My father does.

It's a given that I will go from high school graduation to freshman year of college in a single inhale-exhale.

My dad's retired, but he was in one of the wars. I'm not sure which one because he refuses to talk about it. Except every January 8 and September 2 when he takes out a box of medals and military stuff and polishes it all. Then he puts everything back in the box and hides it in his closet. Under the locked gun box.

When I was little, I wanted to see what was in the box, so I climbed up on a chair and tried to get it down. The gun box slipped and fell. It popped open and the gun landed on the floor beside me.

I ran screaming to my dad and told him I was so sorry, I would never try to see it again, but please don't let the gun shoot me.

He spanked me.

Then he bought a lockbox.

He was career army or navy or air force. I can't remember which. My dad doesn't say much.

He was out by the time I was born, though, so he's never really worked.

My mother never went to college either. She's a professional volunteer. No one organizes more yard sales, bake sales, Bible camps or charity auctions than my mom. I really don't understand where she gets the stamina.

Right now our kitchen table is covered with notepads full of information and deadlines for Save the something. Save the eels. Save the poodles. Save the cannibals. Any cause—that's my mom. Equal-opportunity activist. I pretty much have to be declared an endangered species to get any attention.

Monday nights are bridge nights. Tuesday is a dinner group. Wednesday is arts night—ballet, symphony, theater. Thursday Dad plays poker and Mom plays bunko. Friday night is married bowling league.

Saturdays are for whatever didn't get scheduled during the rest of the week. Sundays they stay home so Dad can watch football. I'm not invited to any of it. Not that I'd want to go, but I'm not invited. Mom says I'm just being self-involved.

Tangent: sorry.

So my parents pretty much decided before I was a known entity that I would, in fact, go to college and get at least one degree. Preferably several so we could all share them.

You'd think Mike would have taken care of this stipulation because he's finishing his thesis on electrical engines and artificial primate brains, or something like that. He has three degrees, half a dozen certificates, a baker's dozen of majors and minors. He's a walking alphabet. But he's a white male, so none of this is particularly astounding.

Unfortunately, he's setting the bar rather high for me. I will have to get at least a master's in something or Thanksgivings are going to be a family struggle over initials.

Dad requests information from every school that has a particularly good athletic program. It's not that he thinks I'm a jock, it's that he really doesn't have a clue what criteria to use. So every week there's another one or two colorful pamphlets from a school whose football team was shown on television or whose basketball team makes it into the tournament.

Once, he was watching an Army-Navy football game and I asked him if a drill sergeant was going to show up in the mail. I laughed. He didn't think I was funny. He forbade me to contemplate joining the service, even as an officer.

Okay, fine. I don't really picture myself as G.I. Jane anyway.

Today there are three catalogs. Duke. USC. University of Miami. I have a tower in the corner of my room where I throw them. I will never see the pamphlets from the small liberal arts colleges I'd actually want to go to.

Not nearly enough time on ESPN for Bowdoin's soccer intramurals.

"Gert, go back upstairs and put on a skirt!" Mom screams at me hysterically.

The pot roast is still frozen in the center. The rice

burned to the bottom of the pan gasps smoke. The meringue pie topping deflates at an astonishing speed. Mom should stay out of the kitchen. Really. Why we couldn't have gone out to a restaurant like we normally do when Mike comes to Sunday lunch, I don't know.

Mike has never brought a girl home. I guess there was one in high school, but that was way before my time.

Today he's bringing a girl. Heather. Hence all the overreaction and bad cooking.

I glance down at myself. Jeans. Shirt. Everything covered. Nothing obscene.

But the look on my mother's face is beyond rational argument. I have no idea why I have to dress up for this. It's not like I'm auditioning for the position of sister-in-law or anything. Frankly, I should be comfortable, and Heather should have to dress up.

I open my mouth.

I close it.

I don't ask. I don't need the answer that badly.

Dad is outside finishing cleaning the gutters and touching up the paint on the trim. Like Heather is going to critique the gutters.

Mike's car pulls up and stops. "They're here," I yell

toward the kitchen. I don't have time to change my clothes after all. Darn and double darn.

"They're early." Mom races to the front window and looks out like I'd make it up to aggravate her. I might have if I'd thought of it.

I look over at the clock on the mantel. "It's two-thirty." The fireplace hasn't worked in my lifetime, but we still have two logs sitting ready to light.

Mom's face comically furrows. Like if her facial muscles convulse enough, she could alter the time-space continuum. "I said to come at three, maybe four. I told him to give me time to get the appetizers ready."

"Well, he obviously knows you squirt cheese on Triscuits and doesn't think that takes very long." I really shouldn't have said that.

"Where is she?" Mom is frantic at the window. She looks like one of those poodles she's trying to save.

"I see no woman in Mike's car." I can't actually see anything other than the back of my mother's head bobbing around.

Mike walks up the sidewalk. Alone.

"Where is she?" Mom shrieks as she yanks open the door. Cooking does not help her mental stability.

"Sick. She's puking at home. Food poisoning from takeout last night," says Mike.

I watch Mom collapse like her pie.

But this means there's an upside. "At least we can go out now. Let me get my coat." I run up to my room before my mother's glare connects with my head and does lasting damage.

rant #4
a weighty matter
(grade a+ assholes)

Okay, so news flash. The school board has decided we will have our weights placed on our transcripts and sent home on report cards along with our grades.

We will actually be graded based on our height-weight proportion. If you're within the normal range, you get an A. Slightly overweight, a B. Overweight but not obese, a C. If you're obese, a D. And if you're morbidly obese, i.e., likely to have a heart attack while in high school, then you fail.

I so wish I was kidding.

Who comes up with this crap?

Principal Jenkins, or Princi-Pal, as he likes us to call him if we see him in the halls. Like that's going to happen . . . moron—came around and did presentations in every freaking first period for the last week.

He said, and I quote: "'Your parents' knowledge

of your overall health and well—being will encourage healthy habits and lifelong fitness.' "

War photos don't convey as much horror as this announcement brings to the students. For a moment we are united against a common foe. Fat, skinny, Pops or Brain, we are one.

I can hear protest chants echoing. "Hell no, we won't go" morphed into "It's not okay, we won't weigh."

Sit—ins have never sounded so promising.

Fat suits will be the new "in" fashion to rage against the system.

Here's the deal: The board members obviously have never been in the bathroom ten minutes before the bell rings in the morning or ten minutes before lunch is over.

Upchuck—i—liciousness, all the time.

We have girls, and I'll go out on a limb here and say boys too, who have more enamel on their fingernails than on their teeth.

Our school isn't special. Not in this regard. Summer camps and relatives and friends on the internet all say the same thing: Be thin or die trying.

They eat the lard of lunchroom food, cafeteria crustiness, then puke it up before it taints the tummy or thighs.

Really, even though I fall into the normal range for weight—if not slightly curvier than some—I think about food. I think about weight. How could I not?

We don't currently have a scale in the school and this bathroom barfing is happening daily. Now they're going to weigh us?

This just in, we're going to have electives on stomach stapling and the South Beach Diet next year.

Humiliating.

Terrifying.

None of their freakin' business.

What's next? Weekly hymen checks to make sure the little darlings aren't doing it?

Spot checks for sperm count? Heaven forbid a guy doesn't have enough swimmers to get the cheer-leaders pregnant by prom.

I don't want to know my weight.

I'm not skinny.

I'm not fat.

I'm just me. Me, who seems to change with the tide and the air and the season. I have enough in-securities, thank you very much, without adding that.

Me, who obsesses over tests because I want to do well. Now I have to obsess over my weight on the off chance I fail to fall into the "normal" category?

Isn't there enough pressure in high school without manufacturing another hurdle?

Why don't the teachers, the parents—hell, the football coaches—all get on the scale during a pep assembly? Let's have the school board strip down and step up.

Princi-Pal should be the first.

Lifelong habits, my butt.

We're all just trying to survive and get the hell out of here.

Where do these people come from?

 six

Adam's waiting by my locker. Uh-oh. What's that face about?

I'm still ticked off he made me sit through Friday night's ordeal. And he's completely clueless that I didn't have a good time. Today, everyone is talking about how Lucas and Sue are exclusive and sexually active. I believe the exact phrase I heard was "pokin' it."

Adam drops his eyes. "So you heard?"

I snort. I can't help it. And Lucas's bed needs a little WD-40, since his room is obviously right above the basement. Of course, the movies were really loud and I had to focus every cell to hear a squeak, but the more I think about it, the more convinced I am.

I raise my eyebrows. Both of them. "You were present Friday night, right?"

"What's that have to do with anything?" He has the nerve to act like I'm speaking Mandarin.

"They went upstairs, like, ten minutes after arriving. Could you not hear the bed squeaking?" I'm playing irate well. Covers the hurt.

He pshaws me. "You've been watching too much reality TV."

He so does not get to pshaw me. "And you've had your head in hand." Puh-lease.

Adam has the decency to look a little remorseful. "I was preoccupied. I'm sorry; was it awful?"

Now what do I say? *Yes, it was horrible and I want you to think about what a terrible friend you were to me every time you see Tim.* "No, I'm just pissy." I'm a good friend. He owes me.

Adam nods. "I'm sorry."

"We've established that. Can we talk about Jenny's new piercing now?"

He exclaims, both shocked and intrigued, "She has a new one?"

"Just change the subject." I don't count Jenny's piercings. That would imply way too much interest in

89

her life and, frankly, she could fall off and I would rejoice.

"Okay. Didn't hear from you yesterday."

"We had a family supper with Mike and his girlfriend."

"How'd that go?"

"It didn't. Food poisoning." Do I need my bio textbook this morning? Crap, I hate hauling stuff around. Don't they know we're permanently injuring our backs?

"Are you sure you're okay?"

I don't want to talk about it. Was I the biggest idiot in the world to think I stood a chance with Lucas? "Fine."

"See you at lunch?" Adam moves off as the bell rings.

I nod, feeling in control of my emotions once again.

Lucas and Sue walk by, holding hands.

I feel serious upchuckedness coming on.

Or tears. Could be tears.

History with Ms. Whoptommy. If I have to hear one more story about the sixties and bra burning and young women not understanding how much easier the world is now—

Hallelujah, she's moved on to the Civil War. We couldn't possibly study history in a linear, chronological way. No, we time travel to whenever strikes her fancy. How fascinating.

You'd think something as relevant as the Civil War could be interesting. But the textbook and Ms. Whoptommy suck all the life from it, and then all I can do is watch poor little history lie there like a wizened grape in the corner of the cafeteria.

The Underground Railroad. Cool. All cloak and dagger and danger. Harriet Tubman. Sojourner Truth. Righteous women.

So why is the entire text devoted to white men who pretty much thought yelling or shooting would solve everything? Oh, I guess they didn't learn anything, because that's pretty much still true.

You should hear my dad yell at a bad football call. The television refs visibly flinch when he gets going.

Lucas and Sue are dating.

What's the point in going on?

It's eyeblinky and tearjerky, but mostly it's just more of the same.

Not really sure how I ever thought Lucas would return my feelings.

It's not like we even remotely revolve in the same hemisphere.

He's a jock.

A Pops.

A delicious specimen of manliness.

Crap. I dozed off.

Group projects?

What did I miss?

No. No. No. No.

I hate group projects.

Please let us pick our groups.

Please let us pick our groups.

Oh no, Ms. Whoptommy has the terrible gleam of power in her eye. The same twinkle Hitler had, I'm sure. She's assigning groups.

Doesn't anyone in authority realize we all do much better work when left alone? That in groups our IQ and handwriting plummet to below elementary school levels?

"Gert Garibaldi." She calls my name. I'm first. Now I just have to pray Jenny is not in my group.

"Stephen Lasko." Ms. Whoptommy spits when she speaks. Okay, Stephen isn't bad. Not real smart, but no serious hygiene issues. Occasional breakout, but then, who am I to throw pus pockets?

"Magdalena Rossen."

Maggie is a good student. Quiet. Looks like we're going to shout at her at any minute. But basically I think she'll be okay. Plus, she's got a rep for doing tons of work because she likes it. Always a plus in group projects.

Ms. Whoptommy pauses with malice. She sends me a look over the top of her mole. I can feel it. She's going to call out Jenny's name. It's perfect, really, when you think about it. I bite down on the inside of my cheek.

"Jenny Cohen." She smiles the name.

Jenny? The horror.

No, I must have heard wrong. Maybe we have a new student named Lenny.

Jenny glares at me and raises her hand like I am the devil. I hate group projects.

Oh, buttocks. I heard correctly.

"I can't work in this group environment. It's not healthy for my self-esteem. May I please work alone or be assigned to another group?" Jenny puts on her most innocent lamby expression.

If swearing was allowed, I'd be effing all over the place right now. That, and any other word I could think of that would otherwise gain me detention.

I'm not a big rule breaker, though. So I'll stick with "buttocks" (like the yummy Brits say "bollocks") and "crap" and "flying monkeys."

"No, Ms. Cohen. You may not have another group assignment." Ms. Whoptommy doesn't even pause to consider Jenny's whine. At least Jenny asked and not me.

Stephen looks crushed, as if Jenny's reluctance to work with us had anything to do with him. He is obviously oblivious to the whole Jenny-and-Gert-hate-each-other thing.

We have five minutes to talk about getting together to do this project. And oh, by the way, we have to do most of the work in one session because Jenny's so busy. I heard the words "cheer," "practice" and "spa" before I tuned her out completely.

Jenny and I square off, facing each other. Predator to predator. I hear a growl.

"My house, Thursday. Four p.m. Anyone have a problem with that?" Jenny tosses her hair in a very practiced move and squints at me.

I am forced to consider. Take on Jenny, or get a lousy grade? I need good grades. It's some sort of chemical imbalance that disables my age-appropriate slackerness. I can't *choose* to fail. Not possible. "Perfect," I say with an icy smile, stabbing her with my mind.

Stephen and Maggie just nod. Frantically. Like they are on their way to the guillotine unless they confess.

"MapQuest it." Jenny writes her address on three rips of paper. "Don't be late. And I'm not providing snacks, so bring your own." This will be a particularly nasty slice of Jenny.

I had better bring the first-aid kit.

And Pringles.

"You're not listening to me." I poke Adam in the ribs.

"Yes, I am." He doesn't take his eyes off the practice field and the football team. He has that glazed donut look.

"No, you're not."

"Yes, I am. You're going on and on about Jenny and Ms. Whoptommy's abuse of your social freedoms."

Oh. I guess he was listening. "I am not going on and on. You make it sound like I'm not getting to the point."

"Gert, yeah."

"Yeah, what?" I think I've been thoroughly insulted.

He sighs. "You do tend to take a while to get to the point. That's all."

"That's all?" *Is he saying I ramble?*

"Don't get all defensive. I just thought you should know that sometimes you get a little carried away."

"It's called passion. Emotion. Friction with life—"

"Sometimes it's called boring."

My mouth drops open. I can't believe what I'm hearing. "Eek."

"I'm not saying it's hugely bad. I'm being honest. You said you value honesty."

"Yes, like I have broccoli between my teeth, not that I'm a boring, ranting lunatic."

"You're not a lunatic. But you do rant. A lot. I don't mind it usually. I thought you should know."

I'm not a lunatic, but I rant so much my best friend feels the need to tell me to shut up? I don't think I wanted to know this. I like my world. I'm right in my world. What's wrong with being right? I cross my arms and look for my mom's car. She's late again.

"Don't be mad." Adam slings his arm around me.

Am I mad, or sad? I thought Adam of all people didn't mind listening to me. If *he* minds, how in the world will I get a boyfriend? Or a new best friend? Am I a freak, or do I embody idiosyncraticness?

rant #5
brilliant minds of today shaping tomorrow (teachers and their whacked ways)

Okay, so I've explained all there is to know about Mr. Slater and his butt twitching. Wonder why we students think "The Red Wheelbarrow" is just a red wheelbarrow? Consider the expertise of the teacher— how seriously can we take a guy who clenches in class?

Let's examine a couple of other brilliant professionals I'm exposed to daily. Mr. Casperelli, the track coach, and poet, who teaches my calculus class. Or more exactly, who breathes in the same room where I'm supposed to achieve calculus osmosis. Mostly he's sharing stories about trying out for the Olympics in 1972, and poems. Lots of poems.

Has he no inner sense of bullshit? Can he not see the snickers, see the faces? Maybe not—1972 was a long time ago. His poems all rhyme; they're bad Hallmark cards. Like those hideously stupid forwards that will curse your life if you don't send them to ten friends immediately.

It's not terribly difficult to get an A in Ms. Whoptommy's history class. It's supposed to be state history, but I think Ms. Whoptommy missed that part in the syllabus she inherited from the last history ho. Our state has no history if the amount of class time devoted to it is any indication. We all simply appeared last week and, woo-hoo, we're a state. When did it become part of the Union? No idea. We're probably part of Canada and no one has gotten around to telling us.

To get a good grade, I basically read the text, write answers to the essay questions printed in the back of each chapter and take the test every unit end. Ignore Ms. Whoptommy most of the time, unless she's looking right at me with those beady eyes and then, well, I have to look back. And hope she can't read my soul using black magic. She has the most amazing mole on her chin. I swear if I look closely enough it has a separate heartbeat.

This is the trouble with school today. I admit, there are a few cool human beings who generally like teens and have knowledge to share—Ms. L for one; the shop teacher for another, though I've never actually seen him so maybe he's imaginary; and

I've heard the AP bio teacher is awesome. But the majority, well, they've forgotten they like teenagers, they've forgotten they ever were teenagers, and we're just simply annoying. Wonder why we give them a hard time? Maybe we're just sending the crap back to where it came from.

seven

Today's lunch is a wash. I don't feel like having the Ramones conversation. Adam is eating with Tim outside in the rare fall sun. I'm betting they have about ten feet between them, and they look away more than they look at each other. But it's progress, right?

What's a girl supposed to do when her best friend abandons her at lunch? I mean, yeah, I'm happy for him, but that'll only get me enthusiastic when it doesn't affect me. Now I'm just pissed about it. I had no idea there was a negative side to Adam getting a boyfriend. I need a boyfriend, or a new best friend. Quick.

Tangent: sorry.

I've never really paid attention to my eyebrows.

I missed that part of the "you're growing up" talk with my mom.

I have no idea they aren't perfect until I'm sitting in a stall during the last few minutes of lunch. I mean, the hair grows and you live with it, right?

Anyway, I'm sitting in the stall and two senior girls come in and stand in front of the mirror and pull out tweezers. FROM THEIR BACKPACKS. There's a definite shout in that. I mean, I knew some girls did it. But I had no idea it's the beauty standard.

I sit there and listen. I almost wish I could reach paper to take notes, but I'd make way too much noise and then they'd know someone's listening. And watching through the crack in the door.

"So, the party was totally cool. Really propped up." Pops senior Emily McTavish peers into the mirror and plucks a few microscopic hairs from between her brows.

"Danny asked me to the movies." Her friend is working the outside fringes of hers.

"I told you opening your eyes up was a good idea," Emily says.

"Well, I mean, I've always waxed the middles, but the arch was completely inspired."

"I know. Take off those." Emily leans over and yanks a couple of runaway hairs from her friend's brow. My eyes tear just watching them.

"Corners to corners . . ." They point from their tear ducts to the front edge, then from the outside point of their eyes to the outside edge of the brow. It's a weird choreographed routine.

". . . Runaway edges . . ." They brush fingers down and smooth the hair left. I've never given much thought to how girls' brows got that arched and fragile look.

I feel a bit like an anthropologist, watching a bizarre cultural ritual not covered in class.

". . . Turn the smile upside down . . ." This, of course, is accompanied by a smile and mimed frowning brows. I'm fairly confident they are referring to the shape of their brows. I think.

". . . And watch the boys go to town." They swing their hips. Face each other for last-minute touch-ups and reholster their weapons.

Then they leave. Which is very good, because I have to check my brows. Breasts I'm aware are a lure. Short skirts. Flippy hair. Giggling.

Eyebrows? Didn't know that.

I must buy tweezers. I have serious work to do.

No wonder Lucas doesn't know who I am.

It all makes strange sense.

Dad drops me off at Jenny's for the group project. This isn't the first time he's been here; Jenny and I were friends in elementary school. Dad pretty much keeled over then; now I notice a slight hitch in his breathing when he pulls up to the door. Jenny's parents are loaded. Their house makes the White House look like a weekend shack.

Stephen gets there at the same time we do. His mom drives an old beat-up Volvo. "Hey, Gert. How's it going?"

I wonder if I should answer or pretend not to hear him until I fix my brows. "Good."

He looks at me funny. "Uh, what do you want to do the project on?"

"We can pick a topic." *Crap, he knows that. He was there. Why am I nervous?* "I think maybe the Underground Railroad."

"Hmm . . ." I have no idea if he's considering the

idea or just doesn't know how to tell me how elementary I am. Or how overgrown my eyebrows are.

"You?" I ask, trying to change the focus from my eyebrows to his.

"One of the prisons. You know, the big one that all those guys died in."

Macabre. Revolting. "Could be interesting." I kinda smile. Not a big smile—an I-don't-find-you-revolting, only-your-idea kind of smile.

"You and Jenny?" Stephen shrugs, the question implicit.

"Yeah, we hate each other."

He shakes his head. "I thought you were friends."

"Like, in fifth grade." I am not going to discuss the fallout with Stephen. A huge stuffed lion, brand-new, that I took to a sleepover. The little bed-wetting issue Jenny's mother didn't mention as she tucked all three of us into a double bed. The ruined lion stinking of pee. The hours Ms. Cohen made me wait to call my parents while she had the nanny wash and blow-dry the dead lion. No apology. No replacement lion. Ancient history.

Jenny swings open the door. "Maggie was on time."

"Nice to see you, too." I'll kill her with kindness. My watch shows we're ten seconds late.

Stephen stutters. He is easily intimidated by Jenny's wrath. I, however, find it stimulating. Perhaps I'll pee on something irreplaceable.

"Come in," Jenny says.

I'm holding a brown grocery bag. I made Dad stop at the supermarket on the trip over. No way in this world am I attacking Jenny on an empty stomach.

Stephen keeps looking at me. Really keeps looking at me.

I wonder if he's analyzing my eyebrow hair pattern. Or do I have a zit growing exponentially? I brush a hand across my face casually. I don't feel anything.

We follow Jenny into a great room. In medieval times it would have been called a ballroom. Lots of chandeliers and a shiny wood floor. It has a TV and sofas. Lots of sofas.

No waltzing going to happen in here.

Stephen is still staring at me. From under his lashes.

I have no appetite.

If Stephen keeps gazing at me like that, I won't eat again until I'm wrinkled.

Maggie rises from a perch on one of the overstuffed islands. "Hi." She's so tentative. I wonder if she ever yells. She's slight and tiny with supershort hair all pixied around her face.

I smile at her encouragingly. She's an ally in this war. Jenny doesn't notice. "Here are snacks." I make a great show of pulling out the junk food. Just in case Jenny feels the least bit bad for being a crappy hostess.

"Cool." Stephen has no trouble digging in.

Jenny scoffs at the food and pulls out her notebook. "Let's decide on a topic and then we can divide up the work."

"When's it due?" Stephen isn't the most attractive person when he speaks with his mouth full.

"We have a week, but aside from the presentation this is the only group time we'll have," Jenny says.

A week in which I have to play nice with Jenny. I wonder if she still has that Barbie she mutilated with the straight pin?

Jenny ignores Stephen. Her right eyebrow is pierced. It's a silver ring that flops when she turns her head quickly. I wonder if she'd appreciate knowing how bull-like it looks? I think if I grabbed it, she'd follow me anywhere. "I'm thinking the Underground

Railroad would be interesting. We could all take different aspects." Jenny looks at Maggie and Stephen.

Stephen's head swivels to me. "Gert said that."

Buttocks, I can't have the same idea as Jenny. "I was thinking more along the lines of Fort Jefferson or Danville. A prison."

Stephen has the audacity to look confused.

I relent. "But the Underground Railroad sounds fine."

Maggie releases a breath. I wonder if she thought we'd come to blows over the topic.

Jenny narrows her eyes at me. She doesn't seem to believe I'd acquiesce so easily.

"It's fine. Underground Railroad," I repeat.

Stephen grabs another couple of cookies. "Good," he mumbles. I don't know if he's talking about the cookies or the topic.

Maggie nods. Have I ever heard a complete sentence come out of her mouth? I must ponder this. She starts typing on the laptop she carries with her everywhere.

"I think our display should be the main routes," says Jenny.

I can't let Jenny dominate. It's just not in my nature. "We could also mark important locations or homes of fascinating people."

Stephen beams at me and nods his head. Thankfully he doesn't speak.

"Okay, Jenny mentioned a couple of topics after class that we might pick, so here's this site I found ahead of time. I think it's what you want." Maggie opens her bag and pulls out a miniprinter. She hooks up a cable, prints out something and hands the paper to Jenny, who passes it to Stephen. I eventually get to see it. A map, showing all the routes plus houses.

"Very nice." I smile at Maggie. That girl is quick on the computer. I wonder how many hours she spent re-searching so she'd have all the bases covered. Or was she merely afraid of Jenny's wrath?

She grins. I think I could really like Maggie. She's cool in a Brain way.

"Okay, so let's start on the backboard." Jenny walks over to a low-slung coffee table the size of a king bed. "I had Maria go get the boards and paints."

Maria is Jenny's live-in. I'm not sure she's still called the nanny, but I think she's the only parent Jenny has ever really had. My mom used to worry about her. Jenny, not Maria. Maria, too, when she was illegal. I think she's papered now. That makes her sound like a dog. Yuck.

We trail along behind Jenny.

"I'll do the routes in black. Maggie, do topographic stuff in greens and browns. Stephen, can you do the houses?" Jenny raises a brow at me. The same one that is pierced so menacingly. "Do something."

"Sure." I need tweezers.

This is going to be a long afternoon.

Maybe I'll add the constellations or quilts, or maybe I'll just paint my nails since Jenny's hogging the whole side of the table.

"How was it?" Adam mumbles into the phone. Salsa music pulses behind his voice. He's going through a Ricky Martin and Gloria Estefan phase.

"No bloodshed." I have my head hung over the side of the bed. If I close my eyes, I can see my heartbeat. "Adam?"

"Yeah?"

"Do you . . . ? Do you, uh . . ." How am I supposed to ask this?

Adam snorts. He picked that up from me. "What? Do I what?"

"Pluck your eyebrows?" I rush out the question and squeeze my eyes tight.

Adam pauses. "Don't you?"

I don't say anything.

"I've never noticed yours." He's trying to make me feel better. But if the gay boy hasn't noticed my eyebrows, that's not real supportive.

I don't respond. The blood in my head is making me dizzy.

"And I notice everyone's eyebrows. Have you seen Mr. Jenkins's? The man has an ape perched above those squinty eyes."

I laugh. It's hard to stay humiliated. "I, uh, never noticed."

"You need to get your nose out of the books more often and read something truly educational like *Glamour*'s or *InStyle*'s beauty tips."

"Now you're sounding girlier than me."

"If the shoe fits. I'll bring a couple with me to school tomorrow. I'll even 'E' you the link to the best tweezers in the world. You can order them online."

"With what credit card?"

"I'm sure you'll think of something."

I have my brother Mike's credit card number. I haven't ever used it, but I have it. This is an emergency. I'm sure he'll understand. "Can you send it now? This requires overnight shipping."

"I had no idea your brows are that bad. I'll bring my tweezers to school tomorrow and pluck you before first."

Okay, that's just too weird. "Maybe you could just give me pointers. I don't want to walk into first all teary eyed. Besides, one more day with reject brows is not going to make or break my year." Would it? Maybe if Lucas and Sue . . . no, I'm sure I'll live.

Adam hums to the music. I can almost see his hips shaking. His parents must be gone, or the music would never be that loud.

"How's Tim?" I dread asking. Because if I ask and the news is good, then we'll spend the next hour dissecting every comment. If I ask and the news is bad, then I'll be happy I get my best friend back, and that makes me the biggest loser in the world.

"Good. He's kinda quiet."

"Not real open?"

"Hard to read."

This I know something about. "It's a guy thing."

"I'm not hard to read." Adam sounds offended.

"No, but then you're not on the far end of the guy continuum, either."

"What's that mean?"

"Think Barbie and the First Lady—they are complete and utter girl. The left side of the line."

"Okay."

"The Rock and Vin Diesel are the right side of the line."

"Okay."

"The rest of us are on the line somewhere between those."

"Caught between The Rock and a Barbie?" Adam laughs at his own joke. I hope he doesn't pull an abdominal muscle.

"I'm serious. I read it."

"You read it, therefore it's true?"

"It makes sense, doesn't it? There are all sorts of girls and all sorts of boys. You're just closer to my end and I'm closer to yours."

"Uh-huh. And how does this have anything to do with Tim?"

"He's closer to Vin. You're closer to the First Lady."

"So?"

Is he *trying* to be dense? "You don't speak the same language entirely."

"Riiighht."

"It's not a sex thing. It's a character thing."

"Sooo?"

"Sex things are different." I hope I sound as knowing as I pretend.

"What do I do about it?"

Oh no, the dread dissection looms. "Tell me about your conversation. We'll figure it out."

He heaves a sigh. His relief overwhelms me. I am such a good friend. "So I said . . ."

While he talks I will work on the class assignment for Mr. Slater: Write an ode with an aba-cde-cde rhyming pattern. Due Tuesday.

rave #2
ode to beauty regimens

Being beautiful is more than genetics or luck.
It is the creams for our faces, the shine powders,
Eye bling on lids, and the brows that we pluck.
For primping and pampering we can spend hours,
Slathering lotions and cleansing and toning,
The pumice and scrubs to polish our feet.
Who makes up these rules and sets this bar?
For there isn't a woman who hasn't been honing
The skills that it takes to walk down the street
Feeling she's the most beautiful from here and to far.

We remove the unwanted hair in pits and on legs,
Though only the truly brave, or insane, wax the
   down under.
The time and energy we use must add up to megs
And all so we attract the desire for plunder.
I'm not immune, for I love the girly glam.
My heaven is a giveaway Sephora, all of it for me.
Though sometimes, just sometimes, with all that I do,
I feel like the world's impossible sham,
For I look in the mirror and only see me,
The ugly girl seeking a beautiful coup.

Nope. Too personal. Besides, it's not aba-cde-cde. Must burn. Think. Think. Ode to what? High school? Homecoming? Driving? The football team. Yep, that's an A+-boring-buttocks-drivelly poem. I'll call it:

"Ode to Our Football Team (Yuck!)."

eight

I have to finish my paper for Slater. English. American lit. Poe and Hemingway. Must do research.

I love the Internet. It's a delicious research tool. Take good ol' Edgar. Did you know he was a necrophiliac? He liked, gulp, banging dead women.

That's just something I don't need to know. It's fascinating in a sick and twisted way, but sadly I can't include the tidbit. Mr. Slater wouldn't see the relevance.

Of course, I have no idea who necrofiliacs.com are; I'm guessing they're looking for a celebrity mascot, or something picking on ol' Edgar. I can't imagine that he really told people he did this.

And it's not like there are sworn testimonies from witnesses. It's just an interesting concept.

See? I can make it relevant. Think of the raven and the beating heart and oh, what about the pendulum being a decomposing body? This is why I find serious fault with American lit. It really should be called American symbols. Because I swear every teacher I ever had sees symbols in the minutiae of a book.

Not that the raven isn't a large bird, but come on. Sometimes a raven is just a raven.

But no, Slater sees symbols everywhere he turns. And there's no way there are that many subtleties authors come up with as they're writing. Don't you think it's simply the answer they give when, say, Barbara Walters interviews them?

"What does the beating heart signify, Mr. Poe?"

"Oh, Ms. Walters, I am so glad you asked that. . . ."

I mean, really.

Take Hemingway's *The Sun Also Rises*. Supposedly one of the great pieces of American literature.

The hero has no dick. It got shot off in World War I. And this, according to Mr. Slater, is indicative of how the entire generation who served in said war felt at the end of the conflict. They were unmanned.

Uh-huh. Well, according to another Web site, Hemingway had serious penis envy. In fact, his was infantile, and he dealt with this by drinking, writing and ultimately killing himself. Hemingway fans all over the world are cringing at the thought. But it's like Freud. He was also seriously whacked and cracked, but a whole profession grew out of his ramblings and symbols. Now, we're not supposed to think that Freud knew anything, but then?

So why doesn't anyone acknowledge that while both are arguably good writers—I mean, who doesn't get creeped out by Poe—they were writers, not mystic scribes? Can't anyone just say, "Nice stories, no symbols"?

Mr. Slater doesn't find my ideas pertinent to any of the class discussions.

So here's what I finally title my paper: "Symbols and Their Meanings: The Work of Two Great American Writers." Again, I can't not get a good grade on the assignment. It's all about compromise. I compromise my intellect to give them what they deem educational so I get a grade that sets me up for more choices in the future.

Boring. Snore. Snooze.

Definitely an A.

Slater's delighted face is revolting.

The man couldn't find a true symbol if it was attached to his ass-ignment with superglue.

Why is it that things stupid people don't understand become deep and artistic? Have you ever noticed that? If no one understands a television commercial, it doesn't stay on the air long and goes to the commercial graveyard in Kansas. But a whisper of art, or genius, or if it has to do with anyone dead— then all of a sudden, it's revolutionary and thought-probing.

I don't get it.

Sometimes stupid and dickless are just that.

It's October. This is important only because it's that time of year. The weird week of chaos championed by the adults as school spirit. It's homecoming week.

Or at least, two weeks from this weekend is homecoming weekend. Which means the PA announcements have started. I wonder if there's an international script where they just insert the right words in the blanks: "Come on, Panthers/Pirates/

Eagles, it's time to show your Bronco/Indian/Devil Ray pride! Homecoming week is fast approaching and it's time to unite with your freshman/sophomore/junior/senior class. There will be class meetings at lunch today in your advisors' rooms. Be there or be an outcast."

And then: "Woo-hoo, go, big blue/red/green/gold, class meetings start in two minutes. Participation is a great way to beef up those college applications. Show your spirit." Crapping buttocks, I have a class meeting to attend. Excuse me . . .

Adam's already at the class meeting. We haven't even talked about our potential involvement in this year's activities. I guess for Adam, who's covertly dating a football player, homecoming has special meaning. Wonder if they'll be king and queen? That I'd like to see. Might even redeem the whole thing. "Thought this wasn't your thing."

I shrug. "College apps. You?"

He pats the chair next to him. "Fan club president." *Aka boyfriend of a footballer.*

Here's the deal. There are two unbelievably cool-looking guys in my class that have dreadlocks. The guys wear them well and make them look cool.

Our class president isn't one of them. He's a very white boy who embodies just about every stereotypical whiteness out there. His name is Jake. He should be on a FOX teen drama. He, alas, has dreads.

It is obscenely difficult to take him seriously, because his hair is wrong in so many ways. He's the class jerkoff, which is why he got nominated. I'm still not sure why people voted for him. But then, maybe they can get past the fake Rastaman attitude, which is an excuse to smoke his parents' weed.

Jake stands at the chalkboard, white chunk of chalk in his grubby hands. "We need a float. Brian's dad has a flatbed truck we can use, so we're meeting at his house Saturday at eleven. Brian's going to be in charge of the design."

That's democracy in action. He who has the truck makes the decisions.

Brian swaggers to the front of the class. This must be a big moment in his life. A room full of people waiting for his wisdom. I can't imagine it happening once he's of age. "The homecoming theme is Under the

Sea: A Magical Undersea Adventure," he reads from a piece of paper. "So, we're thinking of making it look like an ocean, with creatures and mermaids. . . ."

Let's be clear. Mermaids is an excuse to make those of us with breasts wear bikini tops in the middle of fall, during a football game.

"And of course we have to have the mascot in there."

Laura raises her hand. She's so ugly, she smiles all the time hoping no one notices the asymmetry of her features. "We can make seaweed out of crepe paper."

Her sidekick Stacey nods vigorously. "And papier-mâché animals."

Brian's face is comically blank. I don't think he knows his crepe from his mâché. "Sure. Come Saturday and bring stuff."

Oh, wise leaders, why are you such morons?

Jake stands up. "Great meeting, people. Here's a map and directions to Brian's house. Don't be late. We need to win this year!"

I have a flyer shoved into my not-so-enthusiastic hand. I try to smile, but I think it's more a grimace, because Jake smirks at me. He's a jerk.

"This'll be great." I'm fairly certain I sound like a recording.

Adam doesn't even try to be cute about the float. "So that's completely lame."

"Yep."

"You're going with me, right?"

"Of course." What are friends for? In high school they go with you to really lame events because neither one of you wants to go alone. In case the natives get restless and decide to eat you. I've heard of that happening only once, to a freshman who crashed a senior party, so maybe he had it coming. It could also be an urban myth.

Have I mentioned the points we all accumulate as a class for participation in the week's activities? And guess what? It doesn't matter how many points we earn—the seniors will miraculously accrue more and "win" the event. Gee, am I the only one who realizes this?

Must be.

We pour out from the classroom with just enough time left to eat, barf (if you're into that sort of thing) and smooch (again, if you're into that sort of thing).

"Ms. Garibaldi! Oh, Ms. Garibaldi! Yoo-hoo."

I look at Adam. "Tell me *the* Counselor isn't waving her hands and stalking toward me?"

"Sorry, I make it a point not to lie."

"Since when?" I paste my humor-the-adults-in-power smile on my face and turn around.

Adam deserts me. "See you later."

He's probably going to find Tim. Coward.

I, on the other hand, am cornered.

"I am so glad I caught up with you, Ms. Garibaldi. We need to have our annual fall chat."

The Counselor has a policy of sitting down with each and every student once a year to check in and assess both our mental health and our prospects for graduation. I'm going to go out on a limb here and suggest our graduation prospects are a higher priority than our mental health.

"I have a really important—" I don't even get to finish.

"Don't worry, sweetie. I'll write you a note." She captures my sleeve and drags me toward her office. "So, how are you?"

How to answer that question? Honestly? Lie? Tell her what she wants to hear. "I'm good."

She cocks her head like she doesn't believe me.

"Really." I add facial expression and hand gestures. "Really good."

"That's darling. I'm so glad to hear that."

I think she'd have preferred I declare myself suicidal to make her afternoon interesting.

She sits behind her desk and pulls out my file. Or perhaps it's another kid's file; it's not like we're ever allowed to read them. She probably has only one file she uses for every sit-down. "Your grades are exemplary, Gert. I'm very proud of you."

Good, because you being proud of me is what drives me. I'm rolling my eyes on the inside. On the outside, I'm staring placidly like a naked mannequin posed on Fifth Avenue.

"What colleges are you looking at?"

Why this question? I don't know. I have no idea. Is that allowed?

I think I'm breaking a certain parental-adult rule by not knowing exactly what I'm doing the day after I graduate. Of course I'm going to college. It's a given. But where? What? Who? Haven't really gotten that far. I'm way too busy trying to survive.

I rattle off the first few schools that come to mind. "Harvard, Stanford, Dartmouth, Brown, NYU."

She makes a few notes. Probably a smiley face. "That's good. I love you good students who think ahead. It's so important to know where you want to go in life."

Oh no. I gave the right answer but I'm still getting the "know where you're going" lecture. Has she no mercy? I decide to chance interrupting her. "I really do need to get to class."

"Classes will wait. We need to chat."

Oh, buttocks. I like not knowing. *Please don't make me think about this.*

"Gert, you show great promise to be one of the best upperclassmen this fine institution has educated, but I'm worried."

Worried? I'm the great promising worry? I bet she tells everyone they're the best and the brightest. I mean, who does she look at and ask to please end our collective misery by jumping off a bridge? What else can she say, but that we're the promise of the future?

"You aren't much into social activities, are you, sweetie?"

How to answer?

"I'm picky." I shrug.

"Which is good." She vigorously shakes her head. "I'm not suggesting you get involved in activities that aren't on the up-and-up, but school spirit is important. It will help with your development as a truly rounded and gifted citizen of the world."

Huh?

"I would like to see you do more. I worry about my kids who don't fit in, and I just don't want you to feel alone and empty, that your life is meaningless."

Holy-Mother-of-Self-help-Rhetoric, I think I've just been asked if I'm suicidal.

"I'm fine. I gotta get to cla—"

"Of course. Here, let me write a note." She scrawls on a piece of paper. "I was very glad to see you attend the homecoming meeting, Gert. Schools like the ones you're interested in look at more than simple GPA. They want to know you will add to the student life on their campuses."

Now I really must go vomit.

I'm going to be bulimic by the time I leave high school if the adults have anything to do with it.

Five minutes between periods is not enough time to drop books, let alone pee and have a conversation, but Stephen didn't get that memo.

He's waiting by the bank of lockers right smack next to mine. Which isn't weird except that his locker is somewhere on the other side of the building. I've never seen him hang out by mine before.

"Hey," he says.

"Hey." Oh, this is painful. I should ask him something. *What?* I should say something witty and clever. I am so not witty or clever. He's looking at me like I'm going to bite him.

He leans against the neighboring locker like he has nothing better to do. "Um, how's your day?"

"Fine." I want to ask, What are you doing over here? But I don't. I just wait.

"You working on the float?"

"Yes." Has the world shrunk so much that homecoming is now the only topic of conversation?

The warning bell rings. Great, now I'll have to run. Get to the point, Stevie.

"Well, I'll be there, too."

Shocking. "Cool." I nod, paw through my locker pretending to scrounge for something vital.

Stephen steps back, wipes his hands on his jeans. "See ya." He nods and ambles away.

"Sure." I throw my health notebook in my bag and walk in the opposite direction.

I think something important just happened to me. But what?

rant #6
homecoming
(an ancient tradition of humiliation)

Have I mentioned that Casperelli is the sophomore class advisor? He's a Renaissance man.

It's the time of year when the words "home" and "coming" have nothing to do with Eddie McCantly getting caught jerking off in his parents' bed.

Homecoming. With kings and queens and a week's worth of catchy activities.

What is this a ritual from? The Crusades? I mean, football isn't exactly a blood sport. At least not the way our team plays. We haven't won a game in the two years I've been here. Hope is running thin. We're ready to defect to the middle school because at least the peewees have won a few.

Basically the whole week is the lowerclassmen doing stupid things to make the upperclassmen feel special and more evolved. We'll roll eggs with our noses, toss oil-filled balloons at each other, get maimed in the girls' powder-puff game from hell, then parade around at halftime in costume with our special class float.

Of course, then a senior couple gets crowned, sceptered and frocked. The rest of the court get roses and minicrowns so they don't feel left out. We applaud their grand victory over the enemy. Or, as it happened last year, we slunk away with great tales about how next year we'll kick ass.

This year the enemy is Eastside. Their average lineman weighs 250 pounds. Ours, 145. Victory may be more of a mind-set than a reality.

Casperelli makes sweeping statements about school unity and spirit and coming together. Uniting us all in hope of victory.

For a minute there I think he's drafting us for world peace. My mistake.

nine

Here's the deal with health. Ms. Lockreski is our health and consumer ed teacher this year. She's actually a workout junkie–vegetarian–hippie chick, but when it comes to sex ed, at least it seems plausible she's had some recently. Is there anything worse than sex ed teachers who haven't had any since Truman was president? Plausibility, people, please!

Last year, Mr. Fritz subbed on the day they talked to us about sexually transmitted diseases and he called them "Steds" the whole time. It's hard to take sex ed seriously when the teachers haven't even wiggled their stuff in this millennium.

So, Ms. L is cool. She's really pretty, which makes most of the guys blush like crazy, but she also talks straight and doesn't make us draw genitals and label them. You can only color fallopian tubes so many times. It's like being in kindergarten again, only instead of "A" is for "apple," we've got "P" is for "penis." I'm sorry, but at what age does the hormone amnesia set in? When do adultish people forget they had a working brain before they turned thirty-five? Wasn't that what the sixties were about? Do we need another revolution? Make sense, not stupid.

Tangent: sorry.

Basically, Ms. L's cutting-edge philosophy is summed up with "Who cares what it's called if you don't know what to do with it." And yes, that's a direct quote. You can understand why she's one of our favorite teachers.

Of course, heaven forbid we actually have these discussions in mixed-gender settings. If we can't talk about it in the same room with chaperones, how in the world are we supposed to have a conversation after the prom? But no, wouldn't want to make anyone uncomfortable, so they split us up to discuss sensitive topics without the embarrassment of saying stuff in front of the opposite gender. For us, I'm sure, it'll be the period talk for the tenth time; for them I think it'll be wet dreams and masturbation.

I've always wanted to go to the boy talk. What do they do with their sheets? Wash them? Does no one notice? Or do their moms buy seven sets of sheets and just pretend it's normal to change them every morning?

Better still, what about guys who don't change their sheets? Doesn't that get cold? Crispy? Stinky? Stiff takes on a whole new meaning when cotton weave is involved.

These are questions I need answers to. Not the difference between a tampon and a pad and that bleeding is "normal." I know this. I've had my period since I was twelve.

Besides, we started having this discussion when we were in elementary school. Not with the visual aids, mind you, but with age-appropriate puppets. Puppets are scary. Especially the anatomically correct ones. It feels like a violation to the toy world. Toycest or something.

But Ms. L has other plans for the day. No period talk. I'm perking up. This is finally getting interesting.

"Okay, girls. First thing we have to discuss is your general physical makeup. The labia, you all have them, inner, outer. You have a clitoris, aka clit. You have an opening to your vagina, the opening to the urethra and an anus." She sighs. Huffs, really.

"If any of these terms seems vaguely familiar, it's because you've heard them in health class or from your parents or you've talked about them with friends. But if I asked you to draw your own personal genital portrait, I'm guessing very few of you have ever actually looked down there. I don't think you could even get close to reality."

Now I'm interested. A genital portrait? Wow, who knew there was such a thing? Do you sit for that or squat? You'd usually sit for a portrait, but that'd make it a little hard to get the angle right. There are snickers, but not many. We're all pretty much leaning forward, waiting for her to continue.

"Your homework is to get a handheld mirror, like the kind you use to tweeze your brows, sit naked on your bed or bathtub and introduce your face to your crotch."

Really? How's that conversation go? *I've heard so much about you. Only the good parts, I hope?*

"I want you to get acquainted because, ladies, if you aren't comfortable looking at it, then how will you know if anything changes? If you did get an STD, would you know what's different? Would you know if you have a lesion, or discharge, or color change?" She makes lots of eye contact. She has a point. I can't say I'd really know if anything changed. I mean, guys have the advantage of it falling off. Maybe that's gangrene and not gonorrhea, but we women have covert genitalia. Spy stuff.

"Now, the best way to prevent STDs is to not have any sexual contact. This means outercourse, intercourse, petting, oral anything. Is this clear?"

She pauses like she had to say that. "But if and when you do have a sexual relationship, you need to know yourself well enough to direct your partner. At the very least, you need to be comfortable in your own skin."

I think my eyebrows are permanently arched under my bangs. I'm shocked. Not about the subject matter—we've all talked about sex since middle school or earlier, but I've never had an adult actually acknowledge my sexual being. I picked up that term on *Dr. Phil.*

I am a sexual being.

I'm still not really sure if you have to have kissed a boy before you achieve the state of sexual being, but I'll get there.

"Okay, so you look around. In the privacy of your own space—please do not do this on the bus on the way home or request help from your partners. Match the names with the parts. You don't need to draw anything or write any papers, but try it." She waves her hands, clicking her heels against the cement flooring the whole time. It's clear that while she's teaching outside the box, she knows most everyone over the age of thirty-five—again with the hormone amnesia—won't like it.

"Condoms." She holds up a box from Sam's Club. There are enough condoms in there to supply a professional football team for years. Did you see that behind-the-scenes show on ESPN? I had no idea linebackers could be so flexible.

"They all have an expiration date on the box. Freshness counts, ladies. You do not want to have a partner willing to use an expired condom." Ms. L passes out a condom to each of us.

"Open them." We rip the plastic wrappers off, but

it's a bit like hot potato—no one really knows how to properly touch one. Except for Kristen. She knows. She's bored. Scandalous, and slightly awe-inspiring.

I don't think I've ever really played with a condom. In fact, I'm sure I've never played with one. They're kinda like Mom's omelets. Rubbery. Smell funny. Amorphous.

"I don't have cucumbers or bananas, so you'll have to use your imagination." Ms. L toys with hers like a balloon.

"For the rest of the class period, I want you to play with these. Get comfortable touching them, unroll them. It's just plastic. There's nothing evil about plastic." She walks around the rows of desks. I start to expect her to slap the ruler or send us to the principal for having too much fun playing with penile plastic.

Ms. L stops in front of Becky. "Ms. Franklin, do you know what the condom test is?"

Becky shifts in her seat. "Was that in this month's *Cosmo?*"

"Perhaps." Ms. L grins. "The condom test is this. Before you are ready to have sex, you have to be able to walk into a busy store. Any store where there are people around. Maybe these are people who know you, or the store could be a thirty-minute drive from your home."

Giggles and smiles. I think thirty miles is a little too close to the home territory. Make it sixty. A plane ride. An ocean. That'd be good.

"You have to be able to walk in, stroll to the condom section and pick out a box. Then you have to walk to the cashier in the front of the store and purchase said condoms."

I can see a couple of girls nodding their heads. I can't tell if they're agreeing or simply convulsing.

"But." Ms. L flicks her condom onto an empty desk; it makes a lifeless sound. "You're thinking, condoms are the guys' thing, why bother?" She pauses. "Why bother? Because, ladies, you will be the one pregnant. You are the ones ten times more likely to get an STD. You are the ones more likely to be pressured into having sex before you are ready. So, use the condom test. If you're not ready, you won't be able to buy them. If you can buy them without fainting or sweating off your makeup, then perhaps you are ready. This is just an indicator. Say it with me now: the only safe sex is no sex."

We all join in.

I don't know what the boys talked about, but I actually enjoyed today's lesson.

"My tweezers arrived." I pull at the phone cord. Adam is multitasking. I hate it when he does that. I can hear the keyboard in the background.

"You need me to come over and give you a lesson?"

"No, I think I'll just follow the trail of destruction you created after school." I try wrinkling the remains of my left eyebrow. Scrunch it up and then flatten it.

He laughs. "It's not that bad." Audacious boy.

"No." I have to admit my eyes do look bigger, less heavy. "I thought you were going to take off half my face, though." Is there anything more painful? Forget torture—pull out the tweezers and I swear the bad guys will cave. I think there should be a whole new section in special ops training: the tweezering. I think we should have special agents. Think about it—according to CNN, terrorists usually have facial hair. Lots of material to work with.

Adam hums. "They look good. Besides, you get used to it."

"Great. It's an acquired pain sensation. Is there anything worse?" I wiggle my right brow.

"Hmm, yeah." Adam's tone implies I'm reaching the end of the whinability segment of the phone call. "Waxing. Getting kicked in the balls."

Okay, he does have a point, but waxing? He's kidding, right?

"No," I gasp.

"Would you like details?" Dr. Frankenstein cackles into the phone.

"No. Please. No. I'll shut up!" I don't want to know. Really, I do not want to know. He has life experiences I don't want to visualize. Wax and Adam in the same mental frame qualify as criminal.

Adam laughs. The keys stop clicking. Good, I hope he hurts his little fingers, laughing so hard.

I wet a fingertip and smooth the three hairs left above my left eye. "What time are you picking me up for the float?" I ask.

"It starts at eleven—"

"Yeah, but I have my big-city driving trip. We should be back by eleven-thirty, though."

"I'll pick you up at school, then. We'll go from there," he says and starts typing again. IM'ing, no doubt.

Tim? *Don't I get any alone time with my best friend? Must I share him all the time? Let me guess, Tim's practicing at school on Saturday?* I put on my special imaginary Mata Hari spy cap. "Any particular reason you're going to be hanging out at school on the weekend?" I hold my tweezers to the mirror, willing Adam to tell the truth.

"Debate club." He sounds so honest. Too honest.

"That sounds impressive. Almost believable." I snort. Adam doesn't do debate.

Adam clears his throat. I can almost see him looking over his shoulder to make sure his parents don't hear. "There's a Gay-Straight Alliance meeting."

Not Tim. Crap. "That's sadly unromantic." If I have to live a social life vicariously, I need a little bit of Romeo and Juliet thrown in.

"Honest."

Adam wouldn't use the Alliance as an excuse. It's sacred to him.

Shoot. "I know, which is what makes it worse. Can I ask you a question?" *Dare I ask?*

"You need to ask permission?"

I dare. "What do you think of Stephen?"

"Stephen?" He sounds dumbfounded. Not a good sign.

I clarify. "Stephen Lasko."

"Really?"

Could he put more disbelief into one word? What does that mean? "It's just a question." I try not to sound defensive.

"An interesting question."

"Adam." I should never have brought him up. Stephen probably just thinks I'm so unattractive I should be in the circus, which is why he's always staring at me. I'm a freak, and no one has ever loved me enough to tell me. I'm going to have to appear on a national reality show audition to find out just how horrible I am.

"Sorry." He pauses, obviously considering. The silence stretches like spandex on a linebacker's butt. "Good clothes, okay hair, seems decent."

"Oh." That sounds suspiciously like Adam approves. I don't know what I'm hoping, but I think I want Adam to hate Stephen, because then it would make things less complicated. I've never had the flutter feelings for a boy who might possibly have the male equivalent of flutters. It's a little odd.

"He seems cool." Adam clears his throat. The typing stops. "You've finally noticed him?"

"What's that mean?"

"Only that he started following you around last March. And it's October." He has to be telling the truth, because he doesn't lie well.

"No?" How could Stephen have been following me around that long without my best friend mentioning it? Stephen's been following me around? That's flattering. Cool.

Flutter. Flutter. Flutter.

"Really." Adam sighs like I'm boring him with my obtuseness.

"Really?" Has Stephen really been into me for that long? "I have to think about this."

Adam begins typing again. "See you out front of school tomorrow. Don't hit anything, or anyone."

"Very funny." Last semester one of the student drivers hit a parked car, a tree and one of those giant blow-up bunnies on somebody's lawn. All in the same trip. Suffice it to say, we're all glad she's in traction for six months and unable to drive.

Stephen seriously likes me? Really?

I'm flipping through a magazine. *YubbaHubba*, to be exact. *The Insider's Guide to Teenagehood.* Yeah, okay. I'm going to go out on a limb here and say that the editor is in her middle years—Man of the Year is Brad Pitt. No self-respecting teen likes Brad. He's so . . . well, old.

I'm sure he's a nice guy, the whole Jen-Angelina thing notwithstanding. And sure, he's cool with international disasters, but he's not mag fantasy material.

The runners-up are a little more believable but still on the edge of age discrimination. I mean, most of these men have been shaving longer than I've been alive. I could be arrested for ogling them. Not that I'm ogling. Just hypothetically, if I was to ogle. Which I'm not.

Wow. The Gap model has large breasts. I turn my head to get a better angle. Good grief, that's like having a couple of cantaloupe duct-taped to your chest. Not that I've ever done that. I haven't. Honest.

I want to be at one with my body. I'm so far from at one with my body, I'm seeing multiples. Two breasts. Two butt cheeks. Two personalities. How do I go from this stunningly imperfect composition to at one with anything?

Ms. L got me to thinking today. I don't really know what "it" looks like. I mean, other than wiping, and soaping, I haven't really studied it like I have the periodic table. It's not like there are quizzes. It's not on the need-to-know-by-the-time-you-graduate-from-high-school list. The SAT doesn't have an essay question devoted to the topic. The Germans and Japanese aren't ranked each year, in comparison to us, on how well they know their genitalia.

Then there's the name issue. "Vagina" is so unromantic. And really, it's not accurate when that's the inside and the labia are the outside, but think about it. Is there anything in this world with more names?

My grandmother called it "possible." Wash as far down as possible and wash as far up as possible.

My mom, she's kinda past referring to it as anything. I guess when it wasn't scientific terms, it was "hoo-hoo" or "there." As in, has anyone touched you *there*?

But think about it. *Cunt. Pussy. Bush. Mons. Honeypot. Snatch. Beaver. Poontang. Muff. Twat.* I can't resist doing a Google. These are names that get the bad-angry adult faces, and the grounding, and the long talks. Why?

And why is being called one of these any worse than any other name? Shouldn't it be a compliment? A verbal high five—you're so in touch with yourself that you exemplify all that is woman? Makes me wonder who decided they were bad names and how he (because I'm sorry, it had to have been an insecure male who decided) convinced women that having balls is a compliment but being a cunt is the worst thing on earth.

And how do little boys grow up knowing that?

Just yesterday, James Caldango walked down the hall and said, "Sally is such a cunt." Sally got completely bent out of shape. Who told her it was a bad thing to be? I mean, I happen to disagree. I don't think she's a paramount example of womanhood, so I would have suggested an insult more along the lines of "Sally is a total cartoon character." But it wouldn't have the same punch to it. Why?

Why don't we grow up knowing that our parts are okay? When do they go from interesting playthings to off-limits? I missed that chapter in the Life Handbook. Because while I'm not the best of friends with my honeypot, I wouldn't say we're exiled, either.

My tweezers came with a complimentary handheld mirror. Very good timing.

I shove my bookcase over in front of my bedroom door, just enough so no parental units can make an unannounced entrance.

I strip down my jeans and panties. It's a little odd being naked from the waist down. I debate taking everything off, but it's not the warmest day to be spelunking down under in the bush.

The mirror has two sides, one slightly larger than normal and one disgustingly larger than normal. I don't think I want that much magnification.

If asked, could I pick my pussy out of a lineup? That would be a fantastic magazine article. Think about it. Could you?

But I don't think I like the word "pussy." Makes me think of a cat and claws and purring, none of which apply to my parts.

Could I pick my *beaver* out of a lineup?

Don't think "beaver" is really me either. The animal names are odd.

Could I pick my *whatever* out of a lineup?

My pubic hair started growing before middle

school. Just a hair here or there. Now, I think I'm still adding. It's odd. Based on the *Playboy* magazines Adam and I harvested from a box of Mike's stuff in the attic, I thought pubic hair was all neat and tidy.

Mine's not.

It's not a jungle, but it's not the ninth green, either.

Mom's parts aren't too helpful. She's all gray and white and sparse. Like her hair got pulled off with a Band-Aid and never grew back. I haven't really asked if it's always been that way or if she's a reject. Maybe it's because she's so old.

Mine is about the same shade of brown as my eyelashes and brows. Maybe a little darker, or maybe it's just bad lighting. The bedroom isn't lit to make everything easily viewed.

It's a difficult thing to try to compare my curves to other girls' because this angle isn't one we get very often. Boys have it so easy. It's all hanging out and there's no mystery.

Maybe that's why they name their penises. Can't avoid it.

Maybe I should name my twat. What is that, exactly? What's a twat, and who came up with that? It's like a pluot, a plum apricot, but it's not fruit.

Carmen.

Allison.

Raven.

Maya.

I like Carmen. Makes it sound all sultry and spicy. Not at all like the rest of me.

Raven. No. Not a bird. Not a Poe reference. It'd make me think of dead people. And clocks ticking.

Maya. My-ah. Maybe Maya. It's possessive, but still undecided.

"Maya. It's nice to meet you," I say a loud.

The lips, the outer labia, are smooth and hairy at the same time. Not tanned, that's for sure. Pinkish.

I've never understood girls who think they smell bad. I've never smelled bad. It's just like the deep woods meets Bath and Body Works. A little fruit. A little vanilla. A little musk.

Maya is very pink. Red almost.

I wish I had one of those comparison charts, like for buying an appliance. Then I'd know how I compare. It doesn't really matter, I guess, but it'd be interesting.

Like my clitoris. Is it big? Is it tiny? Is it more of a bud than a flower? How does anyone know these things? I understand guys who compare in the locker room. I would too if it was unavoidable.

The holes all seem to be in the right places. I feel like I should make a check mark on some form. Urethra: check. Vagina: check. Anus: check. Woohoo, I'm normal.

Mom's calling. I think maybe I'll have to revisit Maya in the future. It's time for dinner.

I wonder if the parentals will be able to tell I've been hanging out with my new best friend?

I might be able to pick her out of a lineup. I certainly have better odds now. Though I don't think she's going to get arrested for any crimes against humanity.

rant #7
to tame the wild beast
or not?
(what to do with the pubes)

Okay, here's the situation. Obviously, my eyebrows have run amuck. I can only guess that my pubic hair isn't doing what it's supposed to either. Who fell down on the job and left me out of the loop? I think I'll blame Brian Williams or Anderson Cooper. Forget the budget deficit or the latest national disaster: we need an in-depth news report on pubic grooming.

There's even international appeal. How do pubes behave in India? China? Brazil? Norway? And how well do teens know their genitalia in those countries? Can they do genital portraits? Am I the only freak in the world or does someone feel the same way in Cameroon?

Hell, it's a whole TV series in itself. We could have international summits devoted solely to our parts. I bet more than one war was started by someone with pubic-hair issues. Think of the world peace that could come from an open discussion.

How much is enough? How much is too much? What do I do if I fall on the too-well-endowed side of things?

Let's face it, though, it's not like anyone is meeting Maya anytime soon, so let's focus here. Introductions must at least be in the foreseeable future for me to consider taking on that self-improvement project. I'm not ready to purchase my own condoms, let alone have a conversation with "him" about my little curlies. Honestly, I don't have time to care about having nicely groomed pubes because I have my hands full with eyebrow hair.

ten

Here's the deal. I need an attitude adjustment. I know it, but I can do nothing to change. I don't really want to change. It's like having an out-of-body experience—seeing this thing happen in slow motion and being powerless to stop it. I don't really know these people. They could have redeeming characteristics, but come on, they're so easy to categorize.

A Giggle.

A Pops.

A Thing-in-training.

Aka Sarah, Stephanie and Jason.

I am spending my morning with them. In a car. These aren't people I'd put in charge of a stick of gum, let alone my mortal soul.

We should be categorized for driving based on aptitude with complete sentences. It's like one of those kids' pictures titled "What doesn't belong?" I'm squished between an apple, a pear and a grapefruit. I'm the cappuccino. See? One of us doesn't belong in this group.

The looks I'm getting lead me to believe we all feel the same way about each other.

Vipers.

Giggle takes the wheel.

Mr. Fritz tells Sarah to check her mirror, and we all fasten our seat belts. Giggle sucks. Is she driving or playing car croquet? Holy-Mother-of-Brake-Pads, it's not like we're learning to drive a stick. It's a freakin' automatic. There's no need to drive with both feet— at the same time. The right foot, Princess, use only the right one.

I wonder if anyone has ever sued the school district for whiplash brought on by other student drivers. I may break ground. Be a legal precedent.

I'm third to drive. I wait.

Neither the Giggle nor the Thing hits anything too hard. A little scrape with the curb. And a signpost. But I'll live.

My turn behind the wheel. I sit and start the car. I'm tempted to turn on the radio. Lighten things up a bit with a bass beat.

Mr. Fritz starts to wheeze. He does that when he's agitated. Or is he dying? Is this the death rattle? He doesn't look *quite* dead. He's got good color. I don't think I'll have to resort to CPR. I wonder if giving him CPR would qualify me for the special dedication in the yearbook? Probably not.

Tangent: sorry.

So, I adjust my seat. Look in all the mirrors at the lovely gray sky and yellow leaves.

The Pops, Stephanie, makes a face in the rearview mirror.

I step on the brakes a little hard.

After gunning it.

Oops. I mouth "Sorry" in the mirror and feign sadness.

Mr. Fritz thinks I could have stopped longer at that stop sign.

He's wheezing. Again.

I look over at him to make sure he's still alive. He coughs. "Watch the road," he says.

I guess he doesn't care if he dies.

I put my turn signal on and take the left turn like I'm driving a Mercedes roadster that can corner. Okay, so I'm going a little fast. But that's why cars have four tires, right? A few backups for sharp turns?

Giggle just whispers to Thing.

Mirrors are ingenious. I can see the backseat. I whip the wheel to the right and hit the brakes. *Oops, didn't mean to hit that bug.*

"Ms. Garibaldi, you do not have to brake for—what is it you just braked for?"

"There was a small child in danger." Technically true. There's a kid somewhere in the world who right this minute is being endangered. Somewhere.

"Where is the child?" Mr. Fritz looks around like I'm actually speaking about a child, a real child, right here.

"He's under the car." Thing cracks himself up.

"He might be soon," I mutter, and show my teeth in the mirror. It works. Thingy shuts up.

I accelerate on the freeway on-ramp. I'd really like to drive the autobahn. That would be fun. I push on the accelerator, wondering how fast this hunk of junk can go.

"Slow down, Ms. Garibaldi. Watch your speed limit." Mr. Fritz blows his nose.

It's strangely crowded out here. Lots of large vehicles are in my way.

Oops. Good thing that SUV swerved before it hit me. Some people. This state will give anyone a driver's license.

Thingy is trying to put his hand up Giggle's skirt. Wait until I tell Adam. He's always thought Sarah was such a good girl. I guess she and Jason didn't get the memo that backseats are for when you're alone in the car and not when it's occupied by others.

Yuck.

Jason has smelly breath and dirty fingernails. I wonder if Sarah's ever really looked at his fingernails. Talk about contagious diseases.

I hear vague shouting in the background.

"Ms. Garibaldi? MS. GARIBALDI?"

"Mr. Fritz." He doesn't have to startle me.

"Ten and two, please."

"Twelve." What's with the math pop quiz? Doesn't he realize what they're doing back there?

"Your hands, Ms. Garibaldi. At the ten and two

positions." He really should see a doctor about that breathing problem. I think he must have asthma.

Please, Holy-Mother-of-Flatbeds, let me make it through float building. Adam calls me to say he has to make an emergency stop, so he's going to meet me at Brian's.

I ask my dad to take me, and he doesn't seem to mind the interruption. He drops me off at the end of the driveway, even though he really wants to drive all the way up to the front walk. I have to maneuver over him and practically stand on the brake to make sure he doesn't go all the way up. It's dicey.

Brian's house is fairly ordinary, but I don't really want to be seen in the '86 Cadillac. It's such an old car. Dad's cool, though. He doesn't ask any questions I don't have the answers to. Or maybe he's trying to shake off the brake thing. I don't wait around to find out why he's clearing his throat like there's a small dog lodged in there. The whole ride over he talked about Texas A&M and how I should apply there. There was, of course, a football game on when we left the house. *Dad. Dad. Dad. What am I going to do with you?*

I follow the noise to the backyard. Brian's mom must have bought out the wholesale water bottles. She also stocked up on enough chips and dip to feed a small nation during a nuclear holocaust. The picnic table is going to crack and then we'll just have soggy chips and puddles of onion dip. Who buys onion dip for teenagers? Don't they know we have enough to worry about without adding a known bad-breath ingredient to the mix?

Adam's late, so I'm stuck standing here looking stupid and out of place.

"Gert, sorry. Sorry."

Finally. I turn to Adam and say, "Hey. I'm mad at you."

"Sorry. I got stuck mentoring this kid who's thinking about coming out. He's not in a good way. Have they started?" We stand on the fringes watching three hulking Things-in-training throw around particleboard.

I think maybe I'll forgive him. Eventually.

The flatbed is empty aside from Kimmie, who drapes herself in a bikini top on the cab's hood. It's a little cold out here.

"No?" I'm not sure whether they've started. A few clusters of people are talking. Is there a starting gun?

"Come on. Let's see if we can help with the painting." Adam spots Spenser and Clarice and we head in their direction.

Great, I wonder if Avril Lavigne is still alive. I'm sure Clarice will fill me in.

Blah. Blah. Blah. I'll save you the pain.

I'm covered in blue, green and some gook that's papier-mâché birthing fluid.

My hair is stiff with tempera.

"Hey, Gert."

Perfect. Stephen. Couldn't he have said hello this morning before I was completely gooped up? Why now?

"Hi." My smile feels as stiff as my hair. I want to fidget and smooth it back. I don't move, like a rabbit facing down a rabid coyote. Bad visual. Stephen is so not rabid. I hope. Can you catch that from kissing?

"What are you working on?" he asks.

What to say? That's a very good question. It started out as a starfish, but now it looks more like a demented daisy. I settle on a generic title. "Sea creature."

"Oh. Looks good." He's totally lying. Sweet. But lying.

Say something, Gert. Say something. Be intelligent. Be witty. Be— "You working on something?" *Crap.*

He nods like a sage. "Stabilizing the structure so no one gets hurt."

"Oh." *Oh? You can do better than that.* "It would really suck if anyone got hurt."

"Yeah." Stephen looks down at the hammer in his hand. "So?"

Clarice is watching. Avidly. I can tell she's trying to figure out how to get in on the conversation.

"So. How. Are. You." *Breathe. Breathe. Don't freakin' hyperventilate.*

"Good. Good. Okay, so I'll see you round." Stephen backs up a step. Then another. Then he runs into the back wheel.

"See ya." I pretend I'm busy and don't notice. It's like bad breath: I won't point out your clumsiness if you fail to mention mine. It's the teenage code of conduct. But only if you like that person. If you can't stand them, then you make sure they know you know and you spread the word with a few embellishments to everyone who'll listen.

It's the way of the world.

rave #3
freedom on the open road

Is there a more powerful feeling in the world than being behind the wheel of a vehicle, in complete control over life and death? I mean, think about it. We speed around in little metal coffins and multi-task with the makeup and the music and the eating and the talking. And that's just the adults.

I love driving. Being alone with the wind blowing through my hair, my own music ratcheted up to cell-killing levels, my air freshener of piney pleasure dangling from the rearview mirror. I can race along with the rest of humanity, all of us going places and having important things to do. This is the only time in my life I wish I lived in a remote location like Montana or Kansas, with the flat open road begging to be dominated by my impressive driving skills.

Next I will perfect the stopping. Whiplash is an amazing tool most people do not utilize fully. Someone in the car you don't like? Gun and stomp. Say it with me now, "Gun and stomp."

Of course, I've never actually been in a car alone, except in the driveway when I'm waiting on Mom.

eleven

"So, sis. How's it going?" Mike sounds pissed. Why is he pissed? He's the one who's all grown up and moved out.

"Fine." I'm tentative. Careful. I sense a trap.

He's not much for small talk. "So, I got my credit card statement today."

Uh-oh. "That's the postal service for you. Delivery, and all that."

I think he spits into the phone. "There's an interesting charge on here."

"Really?" Maybe he's not really pissed.

"Yep. From www.beautypluck.com. You wouldn't know anything about that, would you?" He's all squeaky.

Who actually spells out the "w-w-w" anymore? "Hmm, now that you mention it—"

"Because I called them to find out, thinking that someone had stolen my card and was making bogus purchases." Mike's voice gets dangerously soprano when he's upset. It always makes me want to laugh.

Mustn't laugh right now. "But—"

He talks right over me. "And they said there was only one thing purchased. A pair of copper-plated, nickel-core, ionic, vibrating tweezers. They assured me they have a lifetime guarantee and can be resharpened free of charge at any time."

He added a few descriptors: they don't vibrate. Our whole family exaggerates. Except me. I tell it like it is.

I must confess. Must tell the truth. "They're top of the line."

"I've heard. I also know they were rated by *Consumer Reports* as a best buy."

Who'd he talk to? The company historian? "Wow, that's a tweezer. Most automobiles don't come with that kind of money-back guarantee. Houses, either. Not plane tickets or—"

"Tweezers."

"Right." What to say? *Do not laugh. Do not grovel.* How do I make him understand? "Tweezers."

"Gert. You could pay for a semester of college for what these tweezers cost." Again with the hyperbole.

"Mike, it was an—"

"You had better not be about to use the 'E' word. Tweezers do not constitute an emergency."

Spoken by the king of unibrows. His people will be sweeping the floor with their foreheads later. "But—"

"Gert. I gave you that number in case you ever got stranded, or were kidnapped, or abducted by sex offenders. Not for tweezers."

He really doesn't understand how important this is. No sex offender would want me looking like this. "But—"

"I can't believe you—"

"Mike, stop, and listen to me. I will pay you for them. I have the cash. I simply couldn't buy them anywhere online without a credit card. I had to."

"Don't even go there—"

"Mike, please, as my big brother, please understand I wouldn't have purchased them if I didn't have to have them." *Grovel, grovel, beg and plead.*

My self-worth plummets from the balcony of a sky-scraper.

Wait.

Listen for it.

Yep, there's the splat.

"Hmm." I don't think he's going to hyperventilate anymore. Thank you, Sally, Queen-of-the-Beauty-Supply, he's run out of words.

"I have the money. I swear."

"And?"

Think. Boy. Mike. What's he want? "And I'll detail your car when you come to dinner on Sunday?"

"And?"

"And I'll be really nice to the girl." I mean, you have to be nice to mentally challenged people—who else would find Mike attractive?

"And?"

"And—" *Crap, what else is there?* "I will never use the card again unless it's an emergency—"

"As defined by the police department or the United Nations."

Great, I can purchase rice for the starving children in Africa, but I can't buy a pair of tweezers. What a brother. "As defined by the police or the UN."

"You will be very nice. And you will make sure that Mom gets most of dinner at the deli instead of cooking it."

Now he goes too far. How am I going to pull that off? I'm quiet too long.

"Or we can send the tweezers back to the military installation they're from."

"Okay." Okay. I'll think of something. Maybe if I unplug the fridge before I go to bed. Maybe that would work. It worked that Thanksgiving my aunts were here.

"And Gert?"

What, we're not finished? "Yes?"

"I had better be able to tell a difference in your eyebrows when I get there."

Faux pas! How'd he find out? I could be building model planes. Tiny model planes. "Eyebrows? Who said anything about using them on my—"

"Heather helped me unravel the charge mystery."

Great, now my potential sister-in-law knows I come from deformed spawn. She won't marry my brother. On the other hand, she's seen his furry face, so maybe she doesn't care. I wonder if he has a hairy back. I haven't paid attention. I should look; I may

169

birth apelike boys if I do the mommy thing. That could be a deciding factor.

"Night." Mike hangs up. I don't think he'll kill me. Of course, I may already be dead when Mom has a nervous breakdown over the upcoming fridge disaster.

But at least I will have a pleasantly surprised expression on my face when they view me in the casket.

Adam's meeting me at our favorite table in the hamburger place. I covet our time here. It's just us. We always come on Saturday nights during the school year. At least we used to. Now we're both so busy, it's more like a special-occasion place.

Saturday nights are pretty free since Adam's parents found out he's a serious sinner. They're Catholic, and they go to Mass Saturday evenings and Sunday mornings. They double up. Adam says it's because he's gay.

Once, he jokingly told them he would be happy to become a Catholic priest, since they seem to get a lot of action in the confessional. The bruise on his cheekbone lasted a week. Strangely, it wasn't his dad who hit him. It was his mother. Splendidly well-adjusted woman.

So, we meet here and hang out and order like six sides of fries over the course of four hours. Sometimes we bring work. Sometimes, like tonight, there's way too much to talk about and so we're workless.

"What are you having tonight?"

"The usual." Fried meat with white marshmallowy carb coating, fries and a diet soda.

"Me too."

"So, Mike found out about the charge."

Adam doesn't even look surprised. "What? You expected him not to read his statement? They do give specifics, you know."

Am I the last to have thought of this? Where have I been? "I know. But he doesn't even wash his underwear, so why would he pay any attention to the bill?" At the time my logic was sound. Now it sounds a little weak.

"He doesn't what?" Adam clears a glob of mustard from his throat.

I guess maybe I've never shared Mike's appalling laundry habits with Adam. "He changes them." I feel the inexplicable need to defend my brother the caveman.

Adam pales. "And?"

"And buys new ones. Throws away the old ones."

"Really."

"Really." I once made the mistake of opening Mike's closet and pawing through it for a sweatshirt to cut up. I never went back into his bedroom.

"Your mom?" Adam chews and coughs. He seems to have a hard time swallowing this information. He even sets down his fries and drink.

"Doesn't do laundry." I've been washing my clothes since I was little. I've only had a few color homicides. Red massacres of white shirts. Pink everywhere.

"I didn't know that." Adam seems surprised. As if there is nothing new to know about me. He doesn't know everything. No one knows everything. I just don't share the most intimate details. I never have.

Adam's face has the strangest hurt expression. "Anything else I should know?"

I think of telling him about my insane crush on Lucas but it feels too personal, too fragile to say out loud. I could confess I'm jealous of Adam spending most of his free time with Tim these days. But then if I say out loud how I'm feeling, I'm definitely a harpy, and he doesn't want to hear it. I wish him being in love could be more convenient for me. "No. We're good."

"Really?"

Why is it he never believes me when I say things are fine?

"Fine." I wish there was something I could say that would help Adam get past this. "How's Tim?" I'm not subtle about changing the subject, but then subtlety never got a girl anywhere, right?

Color flushes back into Adam's cheeks. It's really astonishing how fast he turns red. He mutters.

"What? I can't understand you." I cup my hand behind my ear. A nice touch if I do say so myself.

"I said, he's really a great guy." Adam won't look at me. Why won't he look me in the face?

"Did you have a fight?"

"No, nothing like that."

"What then?"

"You're not going to be happy." He's all sheepish and demure.

"Adam?"

"So, how are the tweezers working out?"

Change of subject? What's going on? "Adam, don't change the subject. Just tell me."

"I—"

"Hi, guys!" Tim's voice blares across my shoulder blades. I don't even have to turn around.

This is our sacred place. Our sacred time. We've been doing this since sixth grade. It's tradition. Us. Just us.

Adam won't look at me.

Tim scoots in next to him and grabs a fry. "How's it going?" Is he an idiot, or is the tension not palpable? I'm going with idiot. I don't answer. I'm afraid if I open my mouth I'll spew fire, or nails, or something equally annihilating, like tears. *Does Adam have no shame?*

Tim looks from Adam to me and back again. "Did I miss something?"

"No," I say, shoving wrappers and ketchup foils into a paper bag. Party's over. Say good night, Gracie.

"Gert." Adam is going to try to make this okay.

I don't want it okay. I want it not to be happening. I stuff my garbage in the bin and swing my pack across my shoulders. My chin is wobbling and my eyes are burning. I keep my head up and shove through the group of people to get outside into the fresh air of the plaza.

"Gertie. Wait." Adam follows after me and grabs my shoulder.

"Don't. I have homework. I'll see you later." I look behind him at Tim, who's come along too. If I glance at Adam, I'll cry.

The outdoor shops and movie theater of the plaza are fair game. But the hamburger joint on Saturday nights? This is our place. It shouldn't be boyfriend accessible. Ever. This is special time. Isn't it? Am I the only one who thinks that?

"Hey, Gert! Great to see you. What are you up to?" Stephen bounds up, oblivious to the tension.

I blink to clear the tear ducts. "Nothing. Much." I paste on a tentative smile.

"I'm going to the movie with my older sister and her friend. Are you going?" Stephen asks. He looks at me like he'd like to stuff me into his pocket and carry me home.

I have only a split second to decide. Choice #1: Go to the movie with Stephen. I don't even know which movie's playing. Choice #2: Stay and try to forgive Adam for inviting Tim. Gee, not hard. I'm not feeling very forgiving. "Sure."

Adam flinches. "Gertie, let's ta—"

"See you round," I say in the general direction of my used-to-be best friend, and walk away with Stephen toward the entrance to the theater. Stephen chats, filling my silence. I don't know if he picks up on it or just pretends not to notice.

The seats are comfy like a hug. I'm in charge of perfect seat finding while Stephen gathers supplies. Oh, Holy-Mother-of-Fake-Butter, I've never been to the movies with a boy. I mean, I've been with relatives and Adam, but never with a boy who might possibly want to put his arm around me or snuggle.

I covertly glance at the snuggle seats with the moveable arms. Too obvious? Besides, I'm not ready to make out in a movie theater. I'm feeling reckless, but not that reckless. I stay where I am.

Stephen hands me Junior Mints and a Coke. A real Coke. He didn't ask if I want diet. Either he doesn't realize diet soda is a girl's best friend, or he doesn't think I need to diet. We mumble at each other. Watch the previews.

It's an action flick with Chris Rock and Denzel Washington as undercover cops. Funny jokes, I think. I mean, I'm not really sure, but the audience laughs a lot. I'm too aware of Stephen sitting next to me. I think I feel waves of body heat radiating off him. We share the mints. I like holding one on my tongue and seeing how long it lasts. Not such a good plan when a boy is unpredictable.

I almost choke when he puts his arm on the back of my seat. I have to clear the chocolate and minty goo out of my lungs. Subtly. Sexy. *Right*.

He doesn't even fake a yawn or anything. Just sort of stretches back. He doesn't touch me too much. So it isn't like he's arm branding me. *Just there*.

He's a really warm guy. Heat waves pulse off his arm onto the back of my neck. I get goose bumps.

I shiver like a mini seizure, which my mother says means someone's walked over your grave.

He turns to me and whispers in my ear. "Are you okay?"

"Yeah, just a thing." Like he could do something to make it better. *Weird*. I laugh it off, quietly, and offer him another mint.

His knee kinda keeps bumping mine. Or his thigh

keeps bumping my knee. Or maybe my knee brushes his thigh. I'm not real clear on who's doing what. It's a little blurry.

Again with lots of people laughing. I sound a bit like a braying donkey. Maybe a little too forced.

He smells good. Like soap and pine trees and boy.

Maybe I'm picking up on his pheromones—those are supposed to be powerful and all giggly-goo. Because I have to say that sitting here next to him, trying to keep my eyes straight ahead while watching him watch the movie, I can almost understand how Giggles evolve into their effervescent selves.

I think the movie is, like, ten minutes long. All of a sudden, people stand up and the lights come on and I still have three-quarters of my Coke and some mints left. I can't remember the last time I didn't eat and drink my movie food before the previews were over. I never have food left at the credits.

Weirdness.

Stephen sits next to me for the longest time. Like neither one of us knows what to do.

I feel much better. I don't know if there are healing powers in boy pheromones, but I'm okay if I never see Adam or Tim ever again. As long as this weirdness with Stephen doesn't end. I don't want it to end.

"So?" Stephen puts his hand on my back as we amble up the main aisle. His sister and her friend walked out eons ago. They'd given us a look—*the* look. You know the look. "Did you like the movie?"

I think he's speaking English. I'm so focused on his hand burning into my back, I have to manually flip the think switch. "Yeah. Of course." *Please don't ask me what it was about. Please don't ask me how it ended.*

"Me too."

Silence suffocates the six inches between us.

"You want to get coffee?" I hear myself ask. I'm being bold. I'm proud of myself, but I have no idea where the balls come from.

"That'd be great." Stephen's smile blinds me. I guess he likes an aggressive woman.

"Good." We walk the three blocks to Starbucks in utter, uncomfortable silence. We both open our mouths at regular intervals but no sounds come out.

He opens the door at Starbucks.

No one has ever held the door for me.

I'm not sure I should like it so much. Is it anti-feminist to like it?

It's all a blur. We drink coffee mixed into lots of cream and sugar and flavored syrups. And look at each other. And look at other things, like the table.

I remember lots of smiling, but that's really it.

Thank God my eyebrows are pristine.

rave #4
boys, men, manly boys and boyly mans

For all their weirdness, I LOVE the penis people. I don't understand them. I can't imagine I'll ever learn their language of grunting and scratching, but I'm going to try. If I have to devote my life to learning, I will do it. I can't explain the compulsion that is me thinking about Stephen now. Or just watching a boy walk by and wondering what is going on inside his head. To have him want to play with my hair and take me exciting places. To touch his amazingly fabulous butt and not be arrested for assault.

Don't they have a distinct smell? When do they start producing that spicy, manly, different-from-me scent? I don't mean the sweaty, take-a-shower odor, but the yummy soap and hint of cologne. The kind of scent that makes me want to inhale in their general vicinity just because I can.

I get fluttery and gooey and cease to function at higher levels. Like I shut down except for feeling things; like the hot rays of Stephen's manliness and the solid rock of femur and muscle under his denim cargo pants. And it's not just Stephen. I lose my breath when I contemplate Lucas and that fabulous new guy on HBO. What is happening to me?

twelve

"Gert. We'd like to talk to you, please."

Uh-oh. What did I do? I can think of nothing that could remotely require the sit-down-serious-talk faces.

Aside from the tweezers, but I don't think Mike would tattle about that. Retribution would be mine. Can he say "Mom's meat loaf?"

"Okay." I perch. There's nothing comfortable about the formal dining room. I don't pretend to understand why we have one, but we do, and it's only ever used for holidays and lectures. It's like the all-festive college-seminar podium. Without the tinsel. Or the dorms.

I really don't know why I'm here.

"We want to talk to you about your birthday."

Why the intense faces, then? They better not sug-gest we rent a clown for the afternoon. The pony for my thirteenth birthday was a tad too much. I will put my foot down on a clown. I will walk to Borneo with nothing but the shoes on my feet if they suggest a clown.

I nod. Rarely is my input actually desired.

"You're turning sixteen, dear." Crapping buttocks, she's using the "dear" word. My mom only uses the "dear" word when she's worked up about something. No visual cues here about whether this is a good serious or a bad serious. I realize labor is painful, but it's been fif-teen years and, like, more than three hundred days—isn't there a statute of limitations on remembering that?

I nod again.

"We think it would be okay if you start dating." She grasps my father's hand like they are affecting nu-clear disarmament.

Do they think I've been waiting for permission? It's not like I've had the opportunity. I didn't even know I'm not allowed to date. *How pathetic is that?* It's never come up before.

"Really?" When all else fails, Mom responds to

questions enormously well. She's like a talking parrot, all head-bobbing and cracker-eating.

"We think that you are mature and responsible, and we trust you."

I think she's been watching reruns of *Dr. Phil* again. Of course I'm mature and responsible. And a total loser since I've never needed permission to date. I hope I didn't just yell that last part out loud.

Obviously not, because they don't twitch. "Okay."

Are we done here? I have to go slit my wrists now.

"We also think you should have your own car. We're not keeping up with your schedule and it would be simpler if you have your own transportation."

Up till now my father remains stoically silent. "But we will expect you to get a job to pay for the insurance and the gas."

The catch. There's always a catch. I'm sure if I wait long enough, they'll tell me I can only date boys who are blond with green eyes, live in Manitoba and like to eat herring raw.

Buttocks! A job? I thought my job was getting the GPA to get into the college of my dad's choice? Now I have to work, too? We're not starving. There's no need to send the children into the field to bring in dinner. Why am I sure arguing is useless? I'm dutiful on the outside and a rebel on the inside.

"Okay," I say.

I'm allowed to drive, but I must have a job to have the car to drive, which is their way of making sure I don't have a spare second of time with which to date.

I'm on to you, parental units. "Aha!"

They flinch.

Crap. I said that out loud.

"We'll talk more after your birthday. But if you choose to drive we want you to be able to start looking for a job now."

"Okay." May I get up now? I now have permission to date. The penis people beating down the door will be thrilled to get that news flash.

A job? What am I qualified for? Nada. Which means manual labor. It's called manual labor for a reason—MANs do it. Not womans. That's the way it should be. I can see my future is full of stocking shelves at Costco or arranging boas at Claire's. Or maybe I can be one of those blue shirts at Best Buy with zits and way too much information about DVD-XYZ-plus-whipped-cream-and-a-cherry-on-top.

Now I can date. I can work, too, but I can date. *Now*.

May I leave this lecture hall before they give me permission to get a lobotomy if I so choose? Because right now it's sounding awfully appealing.

Still haven't talked to Adam. He called and left me a million messages last night. I've turned off the ringer. My fuzzy phone doesn't even vibrate when it's off, so I don't have to wonder what his messages are. I can just delete them.

But I don't. I want to, but I don't delete them, at least not until after I listen to him demand I speak with him and quit acting like a baby squid. I have no idea how a baby squid acts, but I suppose if the shoe fits . . . I'm not over it yet.

Stephen hasn't called. Of course, I didn't give him my number. But how hard is it to look up my number? I'm listed. My parents got me my own phone line when I was, like, five so they wouldn't have to answer the phone for me. Is it my fault Adam and I talk every hour? Or we used to. Not so much anymore. Now he talks to Tim.

I wish I could talk to Adam about Stephen.

I thought I really liked Lucas, but maybe not. Is it possible to like two boys at once, a manly boy and a boyly man? Lucas is more man than boy. Stephen is more boy than man.

It's all very unsettling.

Focus.

History. Think historical thoughts.

Stephen has great hair.

Focus on the looming due date for the project.

Lucas's smile.

Think about the project you need an A on.

It's a little sad how few women were recorded helping with the Underground Railroad. Harriet Tubman and Sojourner Truth, of course, but I'm sure there were Quaker women or farm wives who fed and clothed and did the hard part. The men just shot each other and wrote books about it. There should be a history text called *Laundry: The Untold Truth of the Civil War.*

I wonder if Stephen does his own laundry, or if his mother does it.

Women couldn't vote yet. So they probably couldn't read. And they probably didn't have time to write. Unlike the egomaniacs of the day who wrote down their versions of history, which we're forced to study and commit to memory.

I'd like a history that was everybody's story and not just the winners'. Am I asking too much?

Maybe it's his clothes that smell so good? Maybe it's not him at all. Maybe it's the detergent.

Focus.

I must find a resource. A balanced account of what I want to read.

Aha, Google rocks!

Okay, how freakin' fast do eyebrow hairs grow? Mine are like a Chia Pet—you can watch them sprout. Mucho weirdness. Am I an eyebrow freak? Maybe I have a magic gene, making it impossible to have two eyebrows, nicely arched, of course, for more than twelve hours. Maybe I'm the Cinderella of facial hair. The clock strikes and I must pluck again.

I am going to spend my entire life plucking.

There are statistics about how much time the

average person sleeps and eats and watches TV. But are there statistics about hair removal? I think I must spend more time than average.

Phone's ringing. Maybe Adam will know.

No, I'm not answering.

I'm still not forgiving him.

No matter how much my upper brow looks like the Amazon rain forest.

He needs to apologize to me.

When I'm ready to listen, that is.

Which isn't now.

Nope, I'm busy.

Plucking.

rant #8
together or not at all, right?
(am i allowed to be upset?)

We swore a blood oath in seventh grade to never let a boy come between us. We could hate each other's boyfriends and we'd deal, but we wouldn't let them tear us apart. We promised we'd be support- ive and excited and never be too busy or bored to talk about the boys in our lives. We promised we'd talk about each step of the way and we wouldn't be jealous even if one of us got to date Freddie Prinze Jr. or Usher. We'd be happy for each other if it killed us.

Here's the deal: we made these promises with the full intent of having boyfriends at the same time. How does the single one deal with a one-sided promise? I like Tim fine, but what if I hated him? It's clear I couldn't actually hate him; I'd have to pretend. And I don't want to know how cute he is or about the funny little noises he makes on the phone.

I don't want to talk about Tim all the time. I want to talk about nonboy things in addition to talking about

Tim. It's not fun listening all the time. And Adam? Where'd my best friend go? He was taken over by the invasion of giggly, falling—in—love aliens who alienate humans by narrowing the world to a single person. I don't see him anymore. Not like we used to. We haven't had our Saturday—night fry night for ages. We haven't had a conversation that didn't either start with or lead to an intense dissection of every word and nuance of Tim's.

I am happy for Adam. I really am. But I can't help feeling left out and unwanted. Like I've been replaced by the new model. I am the outdated and unwarranted best friend. I have been exchanged for the new shiny model called boyfriend. And every time I try to bring it up? Adam doesn't understand. He thinks he's balancing this well and that we talk about me sometimes and that he's spending plenty of time with me. And how do you convince someone of something they're sure they understand?

When he asks what I think, he doesn't really want to know. Yeah, I learned that early. I nod and smile and say whatever he really wants to hear if I can figure it out. And he'd dump me in a moment if I said anything bad about the boyfriend. I'm clear on that, too. It's a good thing I have nothing objectionable to add.

So I'm silent and sometimes resentful and I always try to be happy for him. But sometimes I'd like to be happy for me, too.

thirteen

Okay, so here's the deal. I'm wondering about masturbation. Talk about a name that reeks of contagion and a slow, strangulating death. It's not inviting. It must be really easy for boys. I mean, they're always having to move it around, so it's probably not weird to just keep touching it.

Can you imagine trying to walk around with that much flesh dangling between your legs? *Uh, no, thank you.* I'm thinking evolution seriously screwed up on that one. It's gotta be like a wedgie that never ends, and then make it supersensitive. If guys are to be believed, there's nothing worse than getting hit there . . . which makes me wonder why they want big penises. Isn't that just more square footage of hurtness?

Personally, I'd take a small one because it wouldn't get in the way so much and there's less there for serious woundage.

Tangent: sorry.

Masturbation. I have to admit Maya is a little more secretive. Covert and all that.

I haven't ever really tried to make anything happen. I don't know if I'm a freak for not playing with it or I'm a freak for wanting to. Either way, I guess I'm a freak. *That's comforting.*

I haven't played with my clitoris or really felt around for much down there other than the string from when I use tampons, which I don't use often because sometimes they're cool and sometimes they hurt, and I can't ever figure out what the difference is. My parents are out for the evening, a symphony thingy Mom thinks makes her seem cultured and puts Dad to sleep. So I'm taking the visual inspection of Maya to a new plane. I'm going to do a touch exam. Basically, I want to see if I can make myself come. I've never tried.

And I've never accidentally had an orgasm, unlike Stephanie, who'll tell anyone who listens that she comes all the time at riding practice. Perhaps that's why horses are so popular among my peers? Maybe I should try to get over the whole fear of trampling or breaking my neck. At least, I hope I haven't had an accidental "o," because not remembering it would rank at the top of the World's Greatest Disappointments list.

I mean, if I've had one it should be memorable, right? Holy-Mother-of-All-That-Is-Grown-Up, please don't make orgasms a trick played on us by bitter, unsatisfied old people in the media.

I know not to believe everything you see, but how do you know which parts of a movie are a film geek's porn fantasy? Can they possibly be an accurate portrayal when they show women thrashing around in ecstasy? If that's remotely accurate, then I'd know if I had one or not. *Right?*

What if it's like having your ears pierced? You think you're cool until you notice that even the boys have them pierced. So you're not cool anymore, you're just one of the hordes. Maybe I'm the only one who's never had one.

Tangent: sorry.

I turn up the heat. It's a little chilly in here.

Maya's really smooth. Except for the crinkly pubic hair. Which I am so not plucking. Do people pluck pubic hair? Who can answer this without laughing at me? I don't want to pluck anything but my face. I can barely keep up with my eyebrows and people see those all the time.

I let my mind wander to Stephen and the latest romantic comedy starring Jake Gyllenhaal. I pretend Stephen and I are in the movie. Making out in his car overlooking the city. It's a convertible. He has the most amazing mouth. All minty cinnamon, but not too much, just a hint.

I'm lying on Hello Kitty. Mood breaker. This is science, though, so I persevere. I try turning off the lights.

That's nice. I start to get the hang of it.

Very nice.

Yep, definitely never had an orgasm before. Must do that again. I wonder when the parentals are going out next? Must ask surreptitiously.

I can see why adults worry about self-serve. It could be quite addictive. I wonder how often Adam does it. Or Jenny. Or Stephen. Fascinating. Oo, I have a new favorite hobby.

"You've been avoiding me." Adam corners me by my locker. I think about going to first period without my books so I can avoid giving him the opportunity to talk to me. But I chicken out of being that mean.

I miss him, but I won't be bowled over by sentimentality. "You invited a boy to night out."

Adam blushes a deep crimson and stammers, "L-listen to me. I told him we were going to be there, but not to come."

"Right." Like I was born under a cloudy sky. Of course that's what was said, but the wink and wiggle clearly implied *show up uninvited*. I slam my locker door.

"Really. Gert, listen to me."

"I'm listening." I heave a sigh so he knows how grateful he should be. I have a talent for being mad.

"I didn't ask him to come. Tim thought it would be nice to spend time with you, too, so he decided he'd be spontaneous and show up."

Am I really going to believe this? I shrug, knowing full well Adam rarely even bends the truth.

"Gert, I didn't tell him it was a special thing. I didn't make it explicitly clear he shouldn't show up. I wouldn't lie to you. You know that. He feels really bad. But not as bad as I do. I wouldn't do that. I was looking forward to spending time with you. I barely see you anymore, we're both so busy with school."

Shoot. He's right. Adam doesn't lie. It's one of the things I love about him. I nod so he'll continue.

"I'm sorry. I know I hurt your feelings. And next Saturday night, it'll be just us, I promise."

Now I feel like a total skank for making such a big deal about it. "Okay." I should be happy he has a boyfriend. I should be. And I am. I shouldn't feel left out and jealous. Can I be both? Happy and upset?

"Forgive me?" Adam says.

I really want to talk to him about Stephen and coming. *What's it like for boys?* "Okay."

"Now, tell me about the movie with Stephen," Adam demands, motioning for me to hurry since the bell is going to ring any second.

"You saw?" Of course he saw us. I was so hoping to have a witness to my first real date.

"Yeah, we watched you guys walk in together."

I smile. "So, here's the deal. . . ."

It feels good to have my best friend back.

"Ladies, today we're going to talk about—" Ms. L hits the Play button on her stereo for round two of the human sexuality lectures.

Rap blares. *"Let's talk about sex, baby, Let's talk about you and me—"*

"That," she says, pointing to the stereo, "is Salt-N-Pepa. I know they're before your time, but the song is timeless because sex itself is timeless." She pauses for effect.

"Contrary to what you may believe, adults for

generations have been doing everything you are do-ing, or will do. There is nothing new in the world of sex, except new variations and strains of STDs, but that's tomorrow's lecture."

We all kind of smile. Some girls giggle. Others scribble notes like they're transcribing the Dec-laration of Independence. I mean, really—they need notes on sex? Maybe there are bigger losers than me. That's a happy thought. I look around trying to figure out who hasn't experienced an "o" yet.

I feel like jumping up and down and sharing like we used to do in kindergarten with show-and-tell—only what if I'm the last girl in the world to have done it? That would seriously suck. Back to listening.

"You have not reached your sexual peak. You will hit it somewhere in your thirties. Your partner, if he's a he—" (again more twitters) "—will have reached his before graduation from college, and in some cases, high school. The moral of the story is what, Ms. Cohen?"

"Date younger men?" Laughter and hooting. Of course, Jenny answers this question. But she does have a point. What's with the vast difference in peakage?

Ms. L has trouble keeping a straight face. I can tell she wants to laugh too, but she's infected with a moment of adultness. "That's one way to solve the dis-crepancy. Thank you. Anyone else?"

A Pops two rows over raises her hand. "Don't be afraid to ask for what you want."

Okay, could she have shouted "ho!" any louder? I mean, asking for what you want is great, but geez, we don't need to know you do that. *Overshare*.

"Good answer." Ms. L looks pleased.

I squirm in my seat. I can barely make myself come, how the hell am I supposed to give play-by-play to an-other batter?

Ms. L continues. "You are part of the revolution, ladies. Don't be afraid to please yourselves and make sure he pleases you. Men who don't care about making you happy sexually should be tossed to the curb and thrown out with the trash." Her face is really red.

I think Ms. L has a few unresolved issues with men. She needs therapy. She appears dangerously close to passing out. I will her to breathe with my mental telepathy, which has until this point been under-utilized.

I try to picture giving the faceless lover, because I really can't picture Stephen and me actually doing it, instructions.

"No, put your hand there."

"Good, now slide your hip to the right. Your other right."

"Uh-huh, now pass the potatoes . . ."

Really doesn't work.

What happened to the theory that boys are born knowing what to do, and how to do it? I like that much better.

Our presentation on the Underground Railroad is going really well, up until my period starts. Early. So early I'm completely unprepared, without a pantiliner, or pre-period pad or backup tampon. Nothing.

Just me standing in front of the class, and a boy I like, wearing thin khakis and a fitted T-shirt. No jacket. No sweatshirt. *No freakin' way.*

That terrible oozy, gooey, sitting in Jell-O feeling of panic.

Is there anything more mortifying than wondering if you're showing? If there's a bright red badge of embarrassment on your butt?

I want to melt into the floor. I want to flatten myself into a pancake.

Or make myself invisible. Clear. Saran girl.

There's talking, and all I can think about is getting out of here to check.

Sadly, what I want and what I can make happen are two different things.

I neither disappear nor slide to the floor.

I say something utterly random. I must mess up my scripted lines because Jenny throws me the nastiest look and Maggie's face is all concerned. Stephen, bless him, is completely oblivious.

Sometimes boys are good to have around. They don't pick up on things like spikes in estrogen. Girls do. It's like gaydar, only more reliable.

My heart's in my mouth and my pulse races along with abandon. I remember the weeks of endless teasing Susan Fargis endured in seventh grade when her white denim skort sported brown and red splotches.

I don't want to move. I'm hoping gravity will pull it straight down into the seam. No one is going to notice the seam between my legs.

Ms. Whoptommy asks a question about my choice

of locations. I have to pull my head from my ass area; I think I say something adequate. I'm not sure. She nods. So, I guess I'm okay. Jenny breaks in and covers her own butt. It's not like she worries about me, or my grade. She's worried hers will reflect my panic.

At the first possible moment after the presentation, I hurry from class with a lame "I don't feel well."

I rush into a bathroom stall and pull down my pants.

A spot.

Fifteen minutes of worry and hell on earth, and all I find is a little spot.

It didn't even go through my panties.

I hate being a woman.

rant #9 (periods) and rave #5 (self-serve) a woman is a woman is a woman

I hate having a period every month. I'm regular and clockworky, and I loathe the added stress of cramps and bloating and changing soaky-up things on a regular basis. Hundreds of years ago women were pregnant so much they only had, like, nine periods in their lives. Of course, they were dead by thirty, so maybe it's a bad example of how things should be. But really, shouldn't we be evolving? Like ovulating on demand? Pay-per-egg? Why is the period thing acceptable and, say, cancer, for example, isn't? This is a quality of life issue for half the population. I demand research. I demand a government study. I demand a male equivalent of Jell-O squishing womanhood.

On the other hand, I wouldn't want uncontrollable boners for all the world to see. At least women have a covert push button of pleasure no one has to know about. It's like having my own little secret goodness. I've figured out that the seam in

205

Jeans is extremely helpful for in-class activity. Just a little hip twist, a shrug or squirm in the seat and voila, happy time! And I don't have to worry about wearing baggy pants and long shirts and slow dancing with girls while happy. So I'll take being a woman, but I'd like to trade in for a new, improved version of womanhood without the squish. Come on, NIH, where are you?

fourteen

Clarice and Spenser are arguing about Avril versus Alanis. Spenser is old-school angry-femme while Clarice prefers younger—but sadly, no less bitter— artists. I have to wonder why Spenser knows so much about femme rock. It might be his six older sisters; it might be he's been drafted into the rainbow room. I'll have to get Adam's take on the whole identity thing later. Clarice and Spenser are perfect for each other. I wish they'd just figure it out.

Adam saves me a seat at the table next to him. I see no boyfriend lingering in the vicinity. Tim must be working out.

"Where's Tim?" I ask.

Adam finishes chewing on a mystery taco. "Gym. You forgiven me yet?"

"Yeah, I'm over it." I'm not sure I'm over it. I don't know how to do the whole change thing.

"Where's Stephen?"

I shrug. I'm not his keeper. We went to one movie accidentally together. *Right?* I mean, I should not be feeling possessive or anything. But where the heck is he? I look around, trying to be casual.

Clarice chooses this moment to look up from Spenser's sweating face. "Who are we looking for?" She frantically swivels in her seat like one of those teacup rides at Disneyland.

"Stop," I hiss.

She asks louder, "Are we looking for that cute boy of yours?"

My mouth gapes like a dying goldfish's.

Adam rescues me, thank you so much. "Tim—do you see Tim?" *Everything is forgiven.*

Clarice has the nerve to look crestfallen. Like I've ruined her whole day not sharing my innermostest. "Oh. Isn't he in gym?"

The world stops spinning, or maybe just Clarice stops spinning. I'm not sure, but for a minute there I think I'm going to pass out. *My cute boy? Is she serious? Could I have a cute boy? Mine? All mine? I must consider. Do I want one? This one? I've never had to think about other people thinking about me and my potential boyfriend. I don't know how I feel about this. Other than dizzy and slightly nauseous.*

Adam turns back to me. "Sorry," he whispers, and peels a spotted banana. *How can he eat that leopard-banana tree love child?* "Have you talked to him today?"

"We had history together." I debate sharing the whole paralyzing womanly incident. But he won't get it. Boys, even the gay ones, don't understand the whole period paranoia.

"And?" He's unimpressed with my brevity.

"I don't know. We had the presentation and then we sat down and the bell rang."

"Oh." Adam gives me a funny look.

I try to make it up to Clarice and lean in so only she can hear me. "I had the worst thing happen in history."

"What?" Her eyes get really big.

"I thought my period started early."

"Oh no!" She gets it. "Do you need anything? I'm completely stocked, plus Midol and Motrin."

"Thanks, it's okay. I'm covered."

"It didn't . . . you're wearing khakis, right?"

"No, it didn't."

"Good. That's good." She's as relieved as I am.

"What are we whispering about?" Adam leans in and peers at both of us.

"Nothing," Clarice says.

"Girl stuff," I say. I think I could like having a girl-friend. The bell rings. I pick up my tray. "Talk to you later."

"Can you, uh, give this to Tim?" Adam hands me a note.

I snatch it a little too aggressively. Now I'm messenger girl. And here I'm thinking I'm over the whole thing.

I seriously want to read the note. Need to read the note. I mean, why give it to someone if you don't want them to read it? It's why we shoot messengers—they know too much.

Willpower is not my strong suit.

I will prevail.

I will not read it.

That would be bad.

I would be voilating a sacred trust.

I can't help myself.

Women's intuition, my butt. It's because we snoop. It's Darwinian.

Before I can cave to temptation, Tim walks into the classroom. I throw the note at him. Smack him right in the pec with a pointy paper football.

Crisis averted.

But now Tim thinks I want to do him bodily harm.

A girl can't win.

It's Parents' Night at school. The fall nighttime event guaranteed to evoke groans and pleas from every student, be they Pops, Giggles, Things or Brains. It's a given. We all hate our parents invading the school. Without us there, it's just so much worse.

The parents—or guardians, to be all official—get a copy of our schedule and have to find their way around the rat maze. Then the teachers get to lecture on why they are so supremely qualified to mold the minds of the future. I'd really like to hear Mr. Casperelli explain how calculus and track intertwine. Alas, students are not allowed. I don't think it's a Moses-Tablet-rule, but it's definitely a Loser rule. No one shows up with their parents for Parents' Night. At least, I've never heard of anyone who actually attended. It would mean admitting you like your parents and that you like high school enough to show up in the free hours of night.

My parents always dress up like they're going to the White House. It would be so much better for my social stratum if only they were. As it is, they rank as "parents who care," which frankly is worse than not having parents. And they don't really care. It's not like they're around or could name my favorite musical group. They'd bomb the game show based on my life. I have no idea why they think going to Parents' Night makes up for the rest of it.

As if spending fifteen minutes in the same room I spend hours in, with the parents of people I see every day, will somehow imbue them with the perspective and ability to conversate and relate better to me. "Conversate" isn't a word. But it should be. Mr. Slater is always talking about English as a fluid language.

My parents have no idea. They simply can't comprehend school today. They don't understand the Internet, computers, POD classes, the pressure. They had pencils and paper and Wite-Out. Nonprogrammable calculators, kneesocks, no girls' sports and drive-in movie theaters. They might as well have come from Mars in an interplanetary exchange. My mother gets confused. My dad just nods and acts like he knows what's going on. If asked by a teacher or any authority figure what he thinks about something, he'll say "fascinating," then promptly change the subject to football.

You think I'm joking.

I am so not.

Phone. Phone. Phone.

I answer without looking at caller ID.

"Hey, it's Tim."

It's Tim? "Tim?" Why is Tim calling me?

"Yeah, hey, hang on, Adam's on the other line." I hear clicks and breathing.

What in the freakin' free economy is going on?

"Gertie?" Sounds like Adam.

I reply, "Yeah?"

Adam asks, "Tim?"

"We're all here." There's a pause. Like ABC is breaking in with breaking news.

I'm so lost, I don't even know where to start. "What's going on?"

"Tim has three-way calling," Adam says like that explains everything. Like just because I've forgiven them for ruining sacred Saturday, I want to have three-way conversations? *Puh-lease.*

Adam reads my mind. "Tim?"

"Gert, I'm really sorry about the burger place. I didn't know. And I don't want us to not get along. I'm sorry I busted in."

"Oh." He's apologizing. How mature. How adult. *How weird.* "Thanks," I say.

"And?" Adam prompts Tim.

"And, you don't have to say anything, but I thought I noticed you maybe being interested in my brother—"

I can't speak.

Adam jumps in. "I picked up on it too, Gert, and Tim just happened to mention this interesting bit of information, and we thought you'd want to know. Just on the off chance you might, maybe now or in the future, be lusting after Lucas."

I get my breath back. "In the interest of peace talks, sure, I'll listen to anything you might have to say. I am not, however, confirming or denying said lust."

"Okay, well, then Lucas and Sue broke up," Tim says without much fanfare.

"Thank you for telling me that, but I don't really care." *They broke up? They broke up? Holy-Mother-of-Heart-Attacks, that's the most amazing news ever!* I want to dance. I want to squeal.

"Come off it. It's not like it's a big secret," Adam huffs into the phone. He sounds like a damn Chihuahua on a sugar high.

"I guessed. Honest, Gert. It's kinda obvious." Tim sounds sheepish. Only, I don't know him well enough to know if he's telling the truth, or simply covering for his boy toy.

I'm torn. Either I believe them and beg for detail spillage, or I can pretend I am übercool and no one has the slightest idea I drool over Lucas's perfect lips. It's really not a hard one to figure out. "Spill."

Adam exhales. "Tim heard them."

Tim's making all sorts of noises. "She *shrieked* at him."

Hmm. This is interesting. "Shriek. Define shriek."

"Think Loch Ness monster battling the U.S. Marines," Tim blurts.

Interesting visual. I wonder if he needs medication. "Uh—"

"Tell her the conversation part," Adam prompts.

"Oh, well. She's been asking about next year. What happens when she goes to college." Tim imparts this knowledge with a religious zeal.

"Haven't they only been dating a few weeks?" Like I don't know they've been dating thirty-one days, seven hours and a few changes of underwear.

"A month." Tim's boyage is showing.

"She wanted a commitment and he dumped her?" I have to say, this isn't shaping up to sound like Lucas is the victim. I was so hoping he might need a little comforting. I'm good at comfort. I can make brownies, and I've practiced my sincere-thoughtful face every time I pluck, just in case something like this comes up.

"No, she wanted to get engaged."

Okay, there's commitment like going to the winter formal together, and there's commitment like spring break at the family's lake house, and then there's— "As in married?"

Oh my God. I don't have a face for this. Are we old enough for that? I have no words.

Apparently, I'm not the only one mystified, since there's a long open pause.

"Wow." I don't know what else to say.

"Uh-huh. I knew you'd want to know," Adam agrees.

"She didn't just mean she wanted to wear his letter jacket?" I can't imagine the "m" word coming up in conversation. I mean, unless she's— "Is she pregnant?" I have to ask. Though the thought of them, together, like that makes my tummy spin.

Tim chokes. "God no." He says it like he wants to ask what I've been drinking, but it's a reasonable guess. "They haven't." Tim sounds sure.

"They haven't?" I try to keep the glee from perforating my voice.

"She wouldn't even—" Tim breaks off.

Adam clears his throat.

"Wouldn't what?" Dear Holy-Mother-of-Makeup-Palettes, what wouldn't Sue Seymour do? *I must learn.* I repeat, "Wouldn't what?"

But clearly, Tim isn't going to share.

"Go down on him," Adam squeaks.

"Oh." I have to think about this. "Really?" She's a senior. *Can it be that bad?* It doesn't seem like it'd be bad. Maybe a little weird at first, but we're talking about Lucas here.

"So, she's not pregnant. At least not by Lucas," Tim mumbles under his breath.

Now, what's that mean? "She's been busy?" Sue? Perfect Sue? The girl I can't bring myself to hate has a sex life? Where have I been living?

"There's this rumor." Adam fills me in. Supposedly, she and Danny Miller both got drunk at a party. But Danny's spreading the rumor, so please, that's not a report by Brian Williams—that's Geraldo, FOX News at ten.

"I'll believe Danny when I'm stupid, fat and bald," I sputter. I hope to hell I didn't just curse myself. I really don't want to be fat and bald. Stupid might have unexplored advantages.

"That's it."

"Thanks. Really." I feel a bit of a truce blooming in my heart.

Why did I agree to meet Stephen at the library for a midterm prep session? I can't think about history. I am historyless. I am brainless. He has the most amazing hands. Really big. I really should have called Maggie instead. Even Clarice would be more on task, and she's not even in the class.

His fingers are long and thin, but not skinny. They're meaty, but not thick and gross and stubby. I wonder how much bigger his hands are than mine. I wonder if I can work it into the conversation. *Say, Abe's hands were about the size of mine. How do yours compare?* I think that may be slightly obvious. Must think. *Think.*

"Gert?" Crap, he's looking at me funny. Why do I think he said something I was supposed to reply to?

"Stephen?" When all else fails, open your eyes really wide and repeat his name.

He shrugs like my momentary lapse is a mosquito

annoying his left ear. Or is he tic-ing? What do I really know about him?

"What do you think she's more likely to ask on the essay question? Civil War or Napoleon Bonaparte?"

Considering it's a U.S. history class, I have to go with the Civil War for a thousand, Alex. "Good question. That's tough. Maybe we should prep for both possibilities?" I wonder if I can snuggle closer under the auspices of reading his book instead of mine.

"Okay." Stephen's voice is gravelly. I wonder if he's getting a cold, or is this his manly voice? How does one tell? "What are the important things to remember about the Civil War?"

Confederacy. Union. Secession of States. Gettysburg Address. Free the people. Lots of dead. Raping. Pillaging. Stormin' Norman. No, wait, that was the First Iraq War. Ragin' Cajun? No. Is Stephen wearing cologne? I can't tell. "Was it Stonewall Jackson who burned Atlanta?"

"Nah, that was the Detroit Riots. My dad was there." Stephen doesn't even look up. He doesn't have all the neuron hookups in the right place. I mean, he's not the most intellectual of guys, is he? But look at those hands.

"Right. What about Napoleon?" I wonder how long you can date a guy who's not as smart as you. Why do men like dating ditzy CO_2s, but I'm knocking the guy for being less than Mensa material?

Am I too picky? Am I one of those? Destined to live with fifty cats, wear Lycra bike shorts and know the Weight Watchers points for every item in the grocery store?

rant # 10
the rest of my life
(clueless at present)

So, if this was 1800, I'd be dead. Okay, not really, but sixteen was ancient back then. Girls were shipped off to factories, husbands and, well, convents. Ick factor. This brings a bit of perspective when I want to be rational, but come on, times have changed, and who wants to be rational? I'm not even sixteen. My life expectancy is one hundred and fifty. How am I supposed to know what I want to do with the rest of my life?

And isn't high school supposed to be preparing me for the later years? I'm seriously missing the point, then, because so far I've learned the life lessons of plucking eyebrows, never falling for the delicious soccer player and never ever agreeing with Jenny on anything. There isn't career choice in there, college decisions, enlisting. We're too busy. Doesn't anyone get that there isn't enough brainpower left over after we get through the day to think about the future?

There's never enough understanding from parentals

about the whole survival thing. I think they must brainwash attendees at high school reunions so they forget how horrible high school is and remember it fondly. Parents are completely oblivious to the pain and ludicrousocity of these four years. Save me! Please?

fifteen

I will be struck down where I stand, but at least I won't have to eat Mom's meat loaf. I did it. I unplugged the fridge last night, left the door cracked too, in a wicked bit of celery keeper cavorting. Not enough so the light came on and would alert the kitchen staff, i.e., Mom or Dad, but enough so the warm air has a chance to shake its bonbon with the cold stuff. Voilà, takeout.

"Is she pretty?" Mom calls to me while she's frantically dishing up platters full of deli food. She's hiding the Styrofoam in the pantry. Why she can't admit to being a terrible cook, I don't know. There must be a twelve-step program for her. A meeting somewhere with more of her kind in a church basement or senior rec room.

Mike opens the passenger door of his ugly, teeny import-hybrid. If there are gnomes, and they drive cars, they love his car.

"She looks normal." Aside from the world's largest boobs, which look as if the army will sweep in and confiscate them before they blow and do real damage, she looks fairly ordinary. I can't say I've ever really pictured Mike dating. Not dating a humanoid, anyway. Not one with a chest like that.

"Normal?" Mom calls.

"Well, her leather bustier looks like it needs dry cleaning, and her cheek piercings are all infected and oozing pus." I can't resist.

Mom drops something heavy. With sauce. I hear a distinct splash. "Gertrude." How does she manage to add multiple syllables to a two-syllable name?

She'll blame me. I'm not even in the room. "Kidding." She's so easy. Like I'd tell her leather and piercings are normal. Frankly, they're probably more normal than Heather's argyle kneesocks and cable-knit sweater. The checked wool skirt is a bit of overkill. She looks like a walking advert for *Scottish Singles: Roaming Hill and Dale Looking for Love.*

"They're here," I yell as Dad bustles down from upstairs.

"Florida State is winning, Gertie. I really think you should—"

"Think about applying there," I finish the thought. He's not pleased. Why is it parentals want to be all unique and first-person?

Mike is shiny; there's a distinct sheen to his face. And he's red. Really red. Good God, his trousers match her skirt. I feel the dreadful pull to check and see if his socks match, too.

Mom wobbles into the front hall as Dad opens the door. It's not that Mom is fat. She's not, but the tummy-control panty hose she insists on wearing refuse movement. Of course, the hose are from the Carter administration, so maybe Lycra hadn't been invented yet. It's rubber panty hose. No kidding.

"Mother. Father. This is Heather." Mike trips over the welcome mat as he and Heather step inside.

"Michael. How lovely. Heather, you're lovely, dear. Isn't she lovely?" Mom air kisses Mike and wraps her arm around Heather's shoulder. Mom's tentacles are showing; she latches on. I wave a few fingers and give her and Heather lots of room. I can't tell if Mom wants to eat her or adopt her.

Mike looks at me. Clearly, he wants to know whether he'll have to bring up the credit card bill.

"Deli." I grab a few Kleenex and press them into his hand. "Dab." I don't know when I became all older and wiser, but Mike actually looks like he appreciates my presence.

Mike soaks the tissue.

Dad follows behind Mom and Heather at a safe distance, like he'd much rather be upstairs watching the game.

I try to sneak a glance at the clock. Only two minutes have passed.

"You won't believe it," Adam says.

I pick at nail polish that's almost dry. "Try me. I've just lived through the worst three hours on record. Any minute now, Guinness is going to show up to interview us for the longest record-setting meet-the-girlfriend-meal ever."

"Gert, shut up."

Nerve. Adam called me. Need I point that out? I paint my middle fingernail red. I have a system going. Every nail a different color. It has symmetry.

"Sorry," Adam says. "We went out."

"Out? We?" No, we didn't. I distinctly recall no going outage.

"Tim. Me."

"Oh." This is a Tim story. I should have known. "Out?" Haven't they been going out?

"Together. On. A. Date." Adam's ticked.

I can't keep up. "I'm not trying to be stupid here. Haven't you been going out?"

"Not by ourselves. Not touching."

The no touching—that's gotta suck. There's PDA and then there's GDA, and somehow the vast majority of people really don't like to witness GDA. Personally, I think it's the gravity of the affection. I don't mind hand-holding of any mixture, but tongues and spit, regardless of gender—get a room. I'm pretty much an equal-opportunity disliker of anything rated over a PG that's not happening to me, of course.

"So?" I ask, knowing Adam's waiting for a cue.

"We went to Friday's, and then to see that new IMAX on soccer."

Wait. I must have misheard. Friday's and IMAX? We don't have either within an hour's drive. They're way the heck across three towns and fifty burbs. "Adam?" Dare I ask what I'm thinking?

"Yes?"

I dare. "Why so far?" I fear I already know the answer.

"Why else?" He sounds like I've asked for top-secret clearance.

Why else indeed. Less chance of seeing people who might not know the gayage and who might care to try to change their orientation. "Tim scared?"

"Neither one of us is thrilled by the idea of getting the shit kicked out of us."

"No one's beat you up since fourth grade, and let's face it—"

"I know you've said I punched him first, but I didn't. I fell. He happened to be in the way and took offense."

"My point is, it wasn't gay related."

"Yeah, but why push it? We're not ready yet. It's easier this way."

I don't get it. I'd be out all over the place because being gay is so much cooler than being straight. It's interesting. It's a conversation starter. Straight is so boring and unexciting. Plus, I think I'd like beating up stupid people who try to hurt me. Of course, I'd need to learn how to fight back, but I'm smart; I could learn. I should have been a lesbian and Adam should have been straight. We just don't have the right personality traits for our sexual beings.

"You had a good time?" Blue, white, red, black, pink. Other hand time.

"Movie sucked."

"An hour of larger-than-life soccer balls?" I can't imagine.

"Two." The things we do for love.

I sense more to the story with my superior mental telepathy. "So?"

"I kissed him."

Now he has my attention. I put down the polish quickly so I don't spill. On second thought, Hello Kitty might need bleach if I get royal blue nail polish all over her. "And?"

"It was good. Nice. Great." A kiss frying the mind so only little words are possible?

I wonder if I can pull off accidentally dumping out all the polish all over the bedspread. "Details. Leave nothing out."

Phone. Phone. Phone.

"Kathy's Kraft Barn," I answer, sure it's Adam remembering a kiss detail he left out the first fifty tellings.

There's a long pause. Oh, buttocks. I turn the phone so I can read the caller ID. My stomach is now down somewhere around Cape Horn. Stephen. *I will never try to be clever again in my life.*

"Gert, please."

"Hey, sorry. I thought you were someone else," I say, and force a laugh, so I sound witty and not at all insane.

"Oh." He doesn't sound like he's laughing. I'm pretty sure he's having his leg amputated because of the tension and pain on the line. "How are you?"

What do I say? Do I sound interesting, or merely casually bored? "Good."

Holy-Mother-of-High-Heels, help him. I can't

make conversation all by myself. Not without writing out a script ahead of time. And he called me. That's not fair. If he called, he should have the script planned. *Doesn't he know anything?*

"You going to the homecoming game?"

"Yeah. I got talked into being a mermaid." I'm not even sure who cornered me and wouldn't take no for an answer. She had big hair and snapping gum and fake nails. Jessica? Jasmine? Jamie?

"Cool."

"Not really. I don't really go for the whole weird ritual of floats and royalty."

"Oh." He sounds like I just killed his favorite grandmother bare-handed with an emery board.

I rush to repair the damage. Could he be calling about the dance? "Kidding." I laugh fast and giggle a few times. "I really like the school spirit and unity. The coming together. The dressing up." *Okay, stop.* I'm laying it on a little too thick.

"That's good." He sounds relieved. There's some commotion in the background. His mother? A dog? I can't tell. "You want to go to the dance?"

My heart will never beat again. *Cool. Be cool.* Do I want to go? I've always been anti-dances because the idea makes me so nervous I fight the upchuck-i-licious. *Quick. Decide.* I won't eat for a week before-hand, then there won't be anything to puke. Could work. I leap and dance around the room, completely forgetting he's still on the phone.

"Gert?" Stephen says.

"Yes. Sorry, dropped the phone. Fine. That's great." I sit back on my bed and try to keep my toes from tapping. I am a spring that's sprung. I am asked.

"I'll see you at school. We can figure it out later."

"Yeah, sure."

Quick, I must call Adam. I must shop. I must have supersexy dress that Lucas will drool over.

Stephen.

That Stephen will drool over.

I turn off the pink fuzzy lamp with its froufrou light-ing and snap on the fluorescent earth-saving disaster of the overhead fixture. The full-length mirror on my closet door requires Swiffering before it'll give up my reflection. I don't use this mirror unless I have to.

Eyes open.

Brain set to realistic view of reflection.

"Crapping buttocks!" I bite back a scream.

I will never find a dress to cover my butt. Mts. Everest and Kilimanjaro squished together are less conspicuous than my ass. I don't know why I've never noticed this before, but I have the world's largest tush. I require a UN escort for international travel. Maybe even NATO. I have an international incident for my gluttonous maximus.

Why have I never paid attention?

I knew I had booty, but when did it morph into a mountain range? Some people put their pants on one leg at a time. I put them on one butt cheek at a time.

I swivel from left to right.

I try pouting and tossing my hair over my shoulder in a mock red carpet walk.

I wish I'd paid more attention to the damn exercise videos my mother used when I was little. Jane Fonda, where are you now? Oh, yeah, old and all plastic surgery.

Lunges? I try a few with my hands on my hips, across the room and back.

Check the mirror. No change.

Kicks? I do an infomercial-esque pose and strike would-be mugger in his belly button.

Maybe a little tightening.

Squats? Aka men's pliés. Not very attractive, and not much help.

I blow my hair out of my face with a depressed huff. I need a hobby that requires intense physical activity. Hmm . . . nothing interesting comes to mind.

I turn off the overhead and switch the pink light back on. Much better. I no longer look like a plastic surgery nightmare. "No, Doctor, I came in for breast augmentation, not butt augmentation. What's that? I have a size FF rear now?"

Is there any smart black dress in this world large enough to cover my continental butt? Everyone will be looking at my ass. The homecoming royalty will demand different peasants to worship them when they see me coming.

It's useless. I am unfit for human interaction. Maybe there's a Russian gulag for butts like mine.

Must study for the driver's test. I flip open the study book and try to focus.

Stop thirty feet from a school bus? No problem, my butt won't let me get any closer.

I join my parents after finishing the written part of the driver's test.

"How'd it go?" Mom's ready to faint. Dad's intently watching any move I make.

"Well, I wasn't too nervous." *That's a bad sign.*

"That's good, right?" Mom asks.

"That written can be tough," Dad adds.

I nod. "It's no longer a written test. It's an automated computer touch screen. High-tech DMV."

"Oh." They both blink and look at each other.

"There were a few questions I didn't see in the study materials." Like the first sign. It's not in the book. It's a crazy yellow face with a bump for a nose and squiggly arrows for eyes. And the possible answers allowed? (A) Divided highway ends. (B) Divided highway starts. (C) Bumps in the road. (D) You prefer to walk and never want to operate a moving vehicle. I picked (D) for Doomed.

"How long do we have to wait here until they tell you if you passed?" Mom asks.

"A few minutes." I shrug. I'm not smart enough to

drive. I got all cocky with the filmstrips. My head spins with questions and answers. The implied consent law is . . . sex? Don't have sex in a car? Or if you are found having sex in a car, it's consensual? You can't be raped in a car?

Don't follow too closely behind an emergency vehicle. Duh. But could we just talk about why they've stopped using sirens? I mean, you look up and everything's fine, and the next minute there are flashing lights and you have to swerve out of the way. Not that it's ever happened to me, I'm just passing along what I've heard. Sirens are good. You can hear them miles away. Hello? How is traffic supposed to get out of the way if we can't hear you coming?

Tangent: sorry.

"Was there a time limit? Because it seems like you came out very quickly." Mom is trying to be supportive.

"No. But you can't go back and change answers, so once you've touched the screen enough times, it's over."

Dad's reading a pamphlet he picked up from a display rack. "You know the biggest accident cause is failing to see what's going on?"

Duh. Evidence for using the sirens. "Yeah, that was in the study stuff."

There's a huge neon poster on the wall that states there's a big fine for parking in a handicapped spot unless you're disabled. I want to point out the moral implications. How twisted do you have to be to park there?

"Garibaldi? Gertrude Garibaldi?" A very intimidating chain-smoker yells into the waiting room.

I'm not the only nearly sixteen-year-old taking the test today.

I stand up.

"Come with me, please, and we'll schedule your driving test."

"I passed?"

"Did she pass?" My parents crowd in like I've been awarded knighthood. Dame Gert, that's me.

"Yeah. If you'll come with me."

My mom hugs me really tight. My dad just nods his head and smiles.

I follow the-future-lung-cancer-patient over to the scheduling desk.

I can almost see my license now. With a good photo. Not a terrible one that makes me look like a drunken drag queen, which pretty much describes my mother's. There's a shadow of a beard and everything. Really revolting.

Woo-hoo! I passed. I am halfway to driving on my own.

I'm sure the driving part will be a piece of cake. Chocolate cake with chocolate frosting. Sprinkles.

I'm hungry.

rant #11
school spirit sucks

I don't get the dressing up for school spirit days. How does my interpretation of the eighties have anything to do with my school spirit? Or Hawaiian Tropic day? Or dot-com crash day? These don't speak to me.

Here's the deal about school spirit and dances. Basically, I don't have school spirit, and I don't trust the people who do.

Have you seen those nasty reality shows where saggy-flabby prom queen and king wail about how things used to be? How high school was the best time in their life? Hello?

These are people we seriously need to think about shipping north to Canada. Not that Canada is a bad place—they just have more room up there for overinflated-egos-wearing-fake-tiaras. North, very north. I think all the prom princesses from every year, who you know still have the dress hanging in their closets, really need to relocate to the high school in the sky.

The rest of us—maybe even as high a percentage as ninety-five—hate high school. We are the

240

normal, functional, get—us—the—hell—out—of—here group.

    I mean, all fight songs sound the same. No one has interesting color combinations—they're all red and white, blue and gray, green and yellow. Yuck. Serious ick factor. I'd like to go to the school that was Dolce & Gabbana, Dean & DeLuca. Abercrombie & Fitch. Everything we own is a billboard for someone other than ourselves. Tommy. J—Lo. Calvin. Guess. Et cetera. Et cetera. We're ads anyway, right? Why not be honest about it and get up front with the purpose of high school? It's consumerism, people. We're taught for twelve years how to be the best consumers on the planet. Rebel, I say! Rebel— 'scuse me, the latest issue of <u>Lucky</u> just came in the mail.

sixteen

"Hey, Gert. Can I?" Maggie points at the place next to me at the lunch table.

"Sure." I like Maggie. She's quiet, but I think she's authentic. Cool word, huh? It's very existential of me to say someone is authentic.

"What's new?" She looks at me expectantly.

Are we having a conversation? Do we do that? "I passed my written test."

She nods sagely. "Driving. Cool."

"Yeah. You?"

"Not sixteen till April. Really sucks."

Okay, I'm out of topics. I force a bite of cheddar cheese and pickle sandwich into my mouth and chew.

"You going?"

To? She's a little hard to understand. Like she expects us to be thinking the same things. I search and can't come up with a subtle question. "Where?"

She seems surprised by my question. "Homecoming."

Like there's no other locale on the planet anyone would be going to. I nod. I don't know how to mention Stephen without dancing around and that would be embarrassing. He's no Lucas, but Lucas didn't ask me to homecoming and Stephen did.

"Me too." She keeps nodding. "You get asked?" she asks in an almost-whisper.

"Yeah. Stephen." I can't help the smile in my voice.

"Cool."

I flick one of my ultrasmooth brows at her.

She shakes her head. "No. I'm going alone. My mother thinks it'll be good for my social development." Maggie slouches even more into herself.

And I think my parents are bad. I can't really tell if she's buying her mother's crap.

She sighs. "I'm not a cheerleader." As if that explains it all. And really it does. Maggie has the greenish cast of a puppy with food poisoning.

"Your mother?" I ask.

243

"Captain of the squad. High school and college."

"Bummer." That's harsh. "You can hang out with us at the dance. I mean, it'll probably be the whole group even though I'm going with Stephen." *Oh God, I haven't thought that far ahead.* What if he wants to hang out with his friends? Who are his friends? Do I like his friends? What if he doesn't want to hang out with anyone else at all? What's the etiquette? Mine? His? Neither?

Maggie smiles. "Thanks a lot. I really owe you."

I try to look reassuring and invitational. The creepy-crawly insecurities are screaming. I will be hideously ugly. I will throw up in the punch bowl. I will step on his feet and trip on my dress. I don't know how to dance. Wasn't I supposed to learn to dance before high school? Was I sick the day they passed out formal dance training? Maybe I'll get sick for homecoming, too. Ebola. The Plague. Something bad. Something that will make homecoming a nonissue and allow me to crawl back into my closet to hide there for a little while longer.

Mom and I are dress shopping. So much for being the contemporary Typhoid Mary. I am destined to go to homecoming. I'm coming to grips with the nerves, and then every once in a while I panic. I want to go. But I don't.

Mom insists on coming along because it's one of the joys of being a mother. We haven't been clothes shopping together since fifth grade. She needs more joy in her life. She's taking way too much pleasure in this.

The candidates for court were announced at lunch yesterday. I've never seen so much strutting and lip glossing. Girls who haven't ever bumped into me were suddenly all smiley and gooey. It's only slightly transparent.

So Mom is going to try to remember that black is a color, the only color of true evening wear. Don't believe them when they say pink is the next black. Or gray or lavender. So not true. Pink makes everyone's butt look big. Gray is only attractive in business suits. Lavender is, well, lavender. Black is the fat girl's friend, the short girl's friend, the skinny girl's friend and the busty girl's friend. Black is everyone's friend. And frankly, I need all the help I can get.

Mom tries. I have to give her that. Really. She tries almost too hard.

"Stephen sounds like a nice boy, dear."

I haven't said two words about him. "Yep, he's nice."

"And you like him?"

I don't know if I really like Stephen. *How do you know?* I don't. I'm clearly an imbecile. "I think so."

"You're not sure?" She latches on to my uncertainty.

"I don't know. I'm just getting to know him."

"You take all the time you need. There's no reason to rush. How about this, dear? It's really quite lovely." She holds out a pink dress covered in red and orange sunflowers. It's satin and perhaps Teflon. I think it flew around the world as a hot-air balloon.

What to say? What to say? "Wow." I can't lie. I can't bring myself to say anything remotely nice. "Not in a million years." Oh, that comes out harsher than I intend.

"Oh." She puts it back with the defeat of a French peasant.

"It was close." I pat her shoulder. "Just not what I'm picturing." A little less von Trapp curtains and a little more gothic.

"How about this?" She holds up a baby blue organza with silk bouquets of flowers stitched randomly everywhere.

"Closer."

I will not survive this bonding experience. We do this stilted dance of holding up dresses and trying not to be mean for hours. I'm about to capitulate and wear pink just to make it stop.

I see black. Fitted, not too tight, not too I'm-a-woman-not-a-girlish. Velvet with enough stretch to make it easy to move in. I must have. I must try on. I rush to the dressing room, almost knocking an old lady off her feet. I rip off my clothes in the frenzy of finding a dress that could work.

I pull it over my head. Smooth my hand down, keeping my eyes closed until the last moment so I can make an entrance and get the full effect. Oh, I love. It fits like it's made for me. I am pretty. I am beautiful.

I come out of the dressing room and twirl.

Mom looks like she's trying to swallow an elephant's foot. She motions for me to pirouette again.

"What?" I twist and turn. Is my butt too big? No, it fits great.

"Well. It's very grown-up," she says, like that's a bad thing.

"Okay." *This is a bad thing?* I don't look like the lollipop from Wonka-land. This is a good thing. I won't be locked away until the Mardi Gras parade.

"You'll need the right undergarments."

What? "What are you talking about?"

"If you like this dress, you'll need the appropriate underwear."

"Black?" There are moments when I'm certain there was a terrible mistake at my conception.

"We'll need to go to the right store." Mom straightens her skirt as if she needs reinforcements. Any moment now the army will charge in to back her up.

"Huh?" I'm still trying to figure out what she sees that I don't.

"More support, dear, and less give."

Dear God, I've created a monster. She's going to have me wearing control-top hose.

I should have gone with the pink.

The first time I've ever set foot in Victoria's Secret; I can't say I imagined it on my mother's arm. She's scary. Almost like she knows what she's talking about.

"You'll need this." It's black with stakes in it and ribbons. I have no idea where this goes. "They'll need to measure you. And perhaps one of those." She's either waving toward garter belts or fuzzy pink thongs. Who is this woman? What happened to my mother? My mother who wears sweat suits and furry slippers?

We wait for what feels like days on a clerk (whose hair and boobs are way too perky) to finish up with a pair of middle-aged women buying from the Paris Brothel collection. I think one of them is Princi-Pal's wife. Yep, Mrs. Jenkins is at every event. *Too much information.*

"Hi. My name is Candy. Let's go into a fitting room and we'll get you all set up."

Candy? *Right.*

"Are you going to homecoming?" she asks. I swear her teeth do that TV twinkle.

"Uh-huh."

She closes the door behind me, shutting Mom out.

"We'll be out in a jiffy." She whips out a snake of a tape measure and starts doing karate moves with it around my body.

What is she doing with that tape measure? *Overtouch.*

"This your first time?" Candy bubbles.

Am I no longer a virgin? Seems a little invasive, but I wouldn't say I'm experienced now. "Sure."

"Don't worry. I've got just the corset and garter set for you. Let me see your dress."

I'm not worrying. I'm so past the point of worry.

It's not like anyone goes to the football games on Friday nights because our team has talent. Or a winning record. We have a better chance of winning Powerball than we do of sending a player to college on an athletic scholarship. We're not a powerhouse. We're not even a house. We're a tiny little Honey Bucket of a football team.

If my dad could have figured out how to get me to attend a different high school, one with a winning season in the last fifty years, he would have. He's pinned his hopes on my college years.

Okay, here's the deal. I don't know how I came to be standing in the forty-degree evening wearing a cotton sarong and a very small top. A bit of string and triangles that do nothing to cover my very large nipples.

I can't say I'd ever paid attention to nipple size, but then I'd never been in the position to care. Now here I huddle with a couple of dozen sophomore girls, all wanting to show school unity and conformity. They all have a look of blind panic on their faces. I refused to look in the mirror before I left my bedroom. My face, I'm sure, wears the same horror.

I tug at my winter coat. It's down. I really wish we'd picked a winter theme instead of the drowned mermaids because then, at least, I could leave my coat on. I can't watch the game because I'm too nervous.

My parents are in the stands. Along with Mike and Heather. Time has never dragged so slowly. Adam's in the stands watching Tim play. He gave me a smile and wave earlier, but I couldn't get close enough for him to approve of my outfit. Perhaps I should have asked my mom's opinion. Why did I agree to this? I have a bad, bad feeling.

The halftime whistle blows, signaling the start of the parade of class floats around the outside of the football field. Freshmen go first. Then us. Then the upperclassmen, who even have moving parts on their floats.

I'm going to vomit. I'm going to vomit.

I peel off my coat and pile with the others. The freshmen are getting a few claps from their families. They're decked out as a school of fish in our colors. A particularly ADHD school of frantic fish.

I take my place on the crowd side of the float. I'm so slow getting a position I can't even hold a seashell or a creature from the deep against my chest, like some of my more popular peers.

I close my eyes. Pray for the end of the world to hit in the next few seconds.

I'm not that lucky.

"Nice nips, Garibaldi."

Oh, Holy-Mother-of-Areolas. You know that saying about cutting glass? I've never really understood that. Until now.

Krissy leans over to me. "Did you put Band-Aids on?" Band-Aids? What, I'm bleeding, too? Panic must bloom on my face because she rolls her eyes and says, "To cover the cold pucker."

The float begins moving in front of the stands. The scantily clad bodies of the hotties in our class get wolf whistles and cheers from the crowd. Someone shoves me so my feet keep up with the float.

Where was I when the Band-Aids were suggested? How am I supposed to know that? I don't wear bikini tops in October. I don't wear bikini tops ever. *I will never even take off my clothes for a shower now.*

"Wow, Garibaldi," shouts Mr. Neanderthal in his jeans, sweatshirt and Windbreaker.

His friend slaps him on the back. "Yay, Gert."

I do my best to move so my body is half hidden behind an inch-thick rope of fake sea kelp. Not much help. Thank God Stephen is a water boy and not anywhere around here. My parents are clapping and waving. They seem not to have noticed. My dad is scowling, but it's probably because he hasn't seen me this undressed since I came out of the womb.

Who's that waving at me on the sidelines?

Oh buttocks, it's Stephen.

At least he's too far away—

Did his eyes just widen? His jaw definitely drops.

I'm going to suggest the boys around here take off their pants for next year's float. Then we'll see who has the last laugh.

rant #12
off with their breasts

I've never really felt the need to examine my breasts for their conformity. Sadly, it occurs to me these are just another thing to feel insecure about.

Some girls have cleavage. I think a few wear sexy push-up bras. I have none. Cleavage or sexy. Neither. I am without cleavage. Does that mean I have singular cleave? Or clean?

But I do have nipples. What are they for? And why the size discrepancies? Why some tiny nipples, or long pointy nipples, or big honkers of nippledom? Taking the idea they're for feeding babies, does that mean baby mouths are different sizes too? Like little-nip Mom gets tiny-mouth baby or honkin' nips has gigantic grouper-mouth baby? I really don't think baby mouth size can vary that much. So what's with the variance of women's parts? And why can't they just grow when we have kids and go away when we stop? Why can't breasts have a novelty feel to them?

Frankly, they get in the way. Guys look at them. So we look at them. Compare them. Feel inadequate or overadequate based on genetics we have no control over. It's not freakin' fair.

seventeen

Maggie appears out of the crowd in the middle of the field and hands me a T-shirt, bless her. I don't even care that I walk half the track wearing a sarong and a Tinkerbell T-shirt. I grab my coat as quickly as possible and find Adam sitting with Clarice and the gang. I'm not ready to hear from my parentals on my ill-advised display of skin.

Adam puts his arm around me. "I'm so sorry. I should have insisted you pad your top." I guess he doesn't think Band-Aids would be enough coverage.

"Yeah, it's your fault."

"The good news is no one noticed." He hugs me to him.

"Gert, I'm impressed." Victor leers at me and Greg hits his arm.

"No one noticed?" I ask Adam and Clarice, who moves to sit on my other side.

"Do you know studies have shown that human penises are shrinking? They think it has to do with all the pesticides and chemicals in the environment. It has immense ramifications for half the population who say size matters. I mean, think about it, if Victor has children, his boys won't have any penises to speak of. They'll have to put minus signs in front of their fig leaves." Clarice looks meaningfully at Victor's lap.

I chuckle.

"It's true. Victor should really be eating an organic vegetarian diet or his is simply going to shrivel up." Clarice pats my shoulder.

"Gay men are the exception, though, right?" Adam asks, playing along.

"Of course." Clarice nods. "Different animal."

I wave Maggie over to sit with us for the second half and she has an in-depth conversation with Clarice about the Beatles and the Ramones. I don't listen with any interest.

We actually win the game, 3–0. The other team's starting lineup was busted for drinking on the bus over and suspended. They play mostly freshman JV guys. At least the win is the hot topic after the game instead of my breastesses.

We stand and shout and clap with victory. Adam disperses to go find Tim. Clarice and the guys move down to check out the celebration. Maggie goes to find her mother for a ride home.

I walk over to Stephen. "Congrats on the victory." I'm trying to be supportive and interested. Even though I'm still wearing the sarong with my winter coat.

"Thanks." Stephen turns bright red and can't seem to look at me. "We'll pick you up at eight for the dance tomorrow night."

"Right."

He can't even make eye contact. I don't know if my nipples appalled him, or appealed to him. *How to tell?*

"See ya," he says, moving away to clean up towels and water bottles.

I meander to find my family. Thankfully, none of them mention my halftime performance.

Around here we have the game Friday night and the dance on Saturday so people can spend the day together on dates and then go to the dance. Or if you're like me, you use the extra time to get nervous and apoplectic about the evening to come.

Maggie pokes her head out of my bedroom. "Thanks again. Do I look okay?" She tentatively turns in a nano-pirouette. She called in a panic about two hours ago.

"Yes. Absolutely." And she does. "I wouldn't have pegged you for red, but it looks good."

"It was my sister's. She left it in her closet last year from a formal sorority thingy." Maggie's sister is a junior at NYU. My father wasn't impressed when he heard.

"You look good too. Black suits you." She tugs at the strap of my dress. "Whatever you're wearing under that is amazing." I haven't shared my molestation at the hands of a bra fitter. "Your hair needs to be up. Here, let me. I'm good with other people's hair."

259

I'm dubious. She's not a fashionista when it comes to the dead cells. I must hesitate too long.

"Really. Sit." Maggie pushes me gently to the edge of the bed. It's not easy to sit in this dress. Or maybe it's the corset/garter-belt number I have on underneath it. I feel like a cast member of *Chicago*, without the fab body and dance moves.

Maggie scrunches and teases and mousses and I don't really know what else, but my hair looks fabulous when she's finished. Excellent, in fact. Ringlets and curls and up-wisps.

"See?" She steps back, not looking quite so pale. "Perfect. Maybe he'll even kiss you." She smiles.

I think that's supposed to be encouraging. Only it's not. I don't know if I want Stephen to kiss me. My first kiss? With him? He's not—how do I put this? Enough? Is he? He's not Lucas? He's not manly? But maybe he's mine and that has to count for something, right?

I'm so glad I didn't try to eat dinner.

"Ready?" Maggie slips ballet flats on her feet. She told me she refuses to break her ankle just to be fashionable. Besides, the dress is long enough no one will notice her feet.

On the other hand, I purchased the tallest, chopstickiest heels I could find. With pointy toes. They are woman shoes. I've worn them in my bedroom all week trying to acclimate my inner ear to the altitude change and shift my center of gravity up a little. However, I haven't done stairs. "I'll just put these on downstairs." I pick up my shoes and inhale. "Ready."

Instead of paying a radio station to do the music, some boner senior thought his older brother, the community-college genius, should get the fee instead. The brother—we'll call him Less—set up his iPod and itsy speakers along with what is, I'm sure, a completely pirated set of the latest tunes. Kind of. They are his dance mixes. He has aspirations of being a DJ in one of the hot spots three hours away. I think at this point, his aspirations have changed to living past Christmas. I didn't think it possible to butcher hip-hop, but add a little swing and Mozart's ninth violin concerto, and voilà!

The upside, if there is one, is that none of us dances per se, which leads to a serious lack of humiliation on all our parts. I can busta-groove, but in the privacy of my own room, without an audience, not in the latest dominatrix underwear with Stephen's eyes glued to my, well . . . I think he's still visualizing the float attire.

We haven't said more than two words to each other all evening. Maggie's kept up a comforting stream of conversation. I think she talks when she's nervous. Mostly we're standing and looking everywhere but at each other.

A couple of Stephen's friends hover near him while Clarice and the guys appear at Maggie's elbow. Even Spenser has shown up in a suit and seems to be looking at Clarice's aqua strapless with a whole new attitude.

Adam drifts over. "You look mag." He kisses my cheek and grabs Maggie and Clarice's hands and spins them both. "*Magnifique*, ladies."

"Where's Tim?" I ask.

"Talking to a bunch of junior girls."

"You didn't come together?"

"We arrived together, but we're not out this evening. Just two blokes on our own, keeping up appearances."

"What's with the James Bond accent?" I ask.

"It's the suit and tie. It does things to my voice." Adam grimaces.

"Want to hang out here?"

"Sure. Maggie, are you dateless?"

"Yep." She nods and smiles.

"Want to dance?" Adam asks, putting out his hand palm up.

"I'd love to." Maggie regally bows her head. "Just don't step on my feet."

"*Au contraire.* I can dance, but can you keep up?"

"I'll do my best." She laughs, and they wander away.

I hate to admit it, but I'd rather be dancing with Adam than standing here pretending to ignore, but not really, my date, who is pretending the same thing. It's all so painful and awkward.

Less, the DJ, says into a microphone, "A little old-school breakdown for the lovebirds in the room tonight." He turns up the volume on Celine Dion's "My Heart Will Go On."

Stephen grabs my hand and yanks me onto the dance floor. It's like he's afraid he'll chicken out.

Celine? My first real slow dance with a manly boy is to Leonardo's drowning gurgles of endless love on the *Titanic?*

As close as he pulls me, it isn't terribly shocking to feel his hip bones poking into me as we sway and bump unrhythmically to the soaring vocals. We're not speaking. So, I'm thinking—he's not really so skinny that his hip bones should poke me.

Hip bone, singular. Weird. He has one particularly prominent hip bone? Then it dawns on me. That's not his hip. Holy-Mother-of-Hard-ons, I've given a manly boy a boner. It takes some serious investigative hip rolling, but yep, I'm certain.

Wow.

Do you pretend you don't notice? Do you say something? Like, "Gee, is all that for me, or just a physical reaction to my proximity?"

Men have erections, like, every two seconds or something, which leads me to believe there's not much downtime, so are we supposed to be sympathetic? Like if someone was in a wheelchair, I wouldn't point that out, right? Is having a penis just another disability?

Stephen's sweaty. I don't think it's that hot in the gym, but he's sticky, though he doesn't smell bad.

I try to move my pelvis away from his just to give him a little breathing room, but it's like a dog on a leash and comes with me.

How long is this song? I have to gather intel and I can't do that while dancing. Or swaying. Or whatever it is we're doing here.

The end of the song finally comes, that long final note. Stephen grips my hand and pulls me toward the bleachers. He does a lot of dragging and pulling. Is he a true caveman at heart?

His face, green and blue because of the lighting, looks like he wants to talk about serious Mideast peace plans.

We head in the opposite direction from my friends.

He has the most adorable, loony expression on his face. He says something I can't quite lip-read, so I lean closer.

That's when he plants his lips on mine. Drills a home run right there by the basketball banner. It's fast. And fast.

A kiss. Pretty much over before it began. *That's it? That's kissing?*

Hollywood so lies.

Pick up. Pick up. Pick up.

"Gert?" Adam mumbles into the phone.

"Who else? You asleep?" I thought seriously about not calling. For about three seconds, and then I was overcome by necessity.

"Naw, it's only two-thirty." Adam yawns. "I wanted to talk to you anyway. Emergency?"

"Where'd you go? I looked for you and looked for you, but you disappeared."

"I got accosted in the equipment storage room."

"Bad accosting?"

"Tim accosting."

"That's okay, then." I blurt out, "He kissed me."

"Congratulations. Me too."

"When did Stephen kiss you?" I ask.

"Tim."

Thank God, I'm having a hard enough time thinking of Stephen as a sexual being, let alone a bi-being, with my best friend no less.

"How was it?" He clicks on his lamp and I can hear the squint in his voice.

"How was yours?" I don't want to answer yet.

"Good. Once we sort of balanced out the teeth and noses." Much more involved than mine. Did I imagine it? No, because he leaned in to me at my front door. I turned my cheek. His mother was watching from the car. My mother was probably watching too.

"Oh."

"Why? You guys not get the hang?"

"Well . . ."

"Was this when he pulled you over to the state champ banner?"

"Yes," I hedge.

"You weren't there very long. Does he suck?"

Good question. Is the fault mine, or his?

"It was fast." What else can I say?

"Like how fast? California marriage fast?"

"Boy-band fame fast."

"Ew." Adam makes the appropriate and sympathetic noises.

"Well . . ."

"Was it terrible?"

"I wouldn't say that." Who wants to admit their first kiss is horrible? I wanted a sound-track-and-summer-breeze first kiss. I got a Time-Life infomercial first kiss. Then I ask another, more pointed question. "Adam, are we supposed to notice an erection, or pretend it doesn't exist?"

Adam's laughter explodes over the phone line.

"I'm serious."

He sounds like he's choking and all blue from lack of oxygen.

I try not to let his mirth be infectious. I don't think I'm ready to laugh about it yet. "It's not funny."

Apparently, my question is worth thirteen minutes of nonstop chortling. I hate my life.

rant # 13
society of covert genitalia

I've never really had a circle of girls who are my friends. I watch the movies and read the books, and I've never had that warm, fuzzy pinky-swear thing. Aside from the disastrous experience as Jenny's friend, I've relied on Adam. And he's relied on me. Does that make me a loner, or just lonely? It's never occurred to me that maybe one best friend isn't enough. Life is getting so complicated; what if I'm terribly naïve to think Adam will be it forever?

I've always wanted girlfriends, but how do I go about getting a circle of punk? Maybe I'm just defective and don't have the punk aura. I'm secretly jealous of all the giggling masses. What am I missing out on? Adam thinks my questions about guys are funny, and while I don't mind being amusing, being laughed at is not a role I relish. He asked what I was imbibing when I inquired as to the boy smell. Maybe a girl wouldn't laugh at me. Maybe she'd want to know too. Maybe.

It's been so long since I've made new friends, maybe I've forgotten how to do it? Is it like applying lipstick after weeks of living in the jungle? Must try. I'm seriously pathetic.

⟨sheep drawing⟩ eighteen

My sixteenth birthday is Thursday. The big one-
six. The first birthday that changes my place in society. No longer am I just a kid. Or just a teen. I'm a
driver. Or I will be when I pass my driving test this
week. But first we must celebrate me. Mom informs me
it's not convenient for the fam to all celebrate on
Thursday, the actual date of my birth, so we're doing a
relative thing at Romano's for lunch today. Since it's
just the parentals, Mike and probably Heather, I'm not
sure who has the scheduling conflict. It's not me.

I wasn't consulted about getting together the day
after the homecoming dance. It's not like I was out all
night, but I spent sleep time listening to Adam chortle
on the phone. Then he called Tim. They both called

back and laughed at me. They teased me about introducing myself to said erection like I'd met him at a party. And while it's an honest question, I'm still not clear about the answer.

Where's a girl supposed to learn this stuff? There's no way I'm asking my father or my way-older brother. I ask my best friend and he can't catch his breath laughing so hard. Who am I supposed to ask? Butt-twitching Slater or the FedEx man? Maybe Princi-Pal Jenkins can shed light on proper erector etiquette.

Tangent: sorry.

Back to the birthday. The good news is Mom won't be baking any bricks with gluey icing. Mike and Heather will be there to take the pressure off me as well.

The sixteenth birthday is freaking out the parentals. They are spending lots of time staring at me. Just looking. Just being creepy.

Dad's slightly more stoic than usual and Mom more weepy. It's eerie.

Sixteen. I'm turning sixteen. *Wow.* Think about what I'm leaving behind: crayons, pink, Barbies—okay, I'm over it. Nostalgia is not me.

This is mega-überiffic.

Mom knocks on the bedroom door at eleven o'clock. "Gertrude dear, it's time to get up."

" 'Kay." I think I got about thirty minutes of sleep riddled with giant dancing penises. Nightmare. I don't much care what I wear, but Mom has never missed a Kodak moment in her life. In fact, she has boxes of photographs no one has ever actually looked at. The spare bedroom is full of them. And her scrapbooking supplies. I've never seen a book or a completed page, but she's prepared on the off chance we have to glue and crop our way out of World War III.

We are meeting Mike and Heather at the restaurant. Heather's still new and though the parentals have talked it to death, none of us is sure if she's a future fam or just passing through. I vote for future fam since she seems normal and Mike has never brought a girl to stuff like this.

Mike and Heather are late. Nothing ticks Dad off more than unpunctuality. He paces. I merely play with sugar packets and rip a piece of paper into tinier and tinier shreds. Mom is reading a book about fabulous fund-raisers.

"Sorry. Sorry. The car battery—we had to jump it." Mike rushes in, towing Heather by the hand.

They look rather rumpled. Not at all like they had car trouble, but more like they jumped each other. Mike winks at me.

"Not on my birthday." I stick my tongue out at Mike as he messes up my hair. They had sex on my birthday. Ew. Holy-Mother-of-the-DVD, I will never get that visual out of my head. *Rude. Rude. Rude.*

"Car trouble?" My mom doesn't follow.

Maybe I can ask Heather the erection question. Maybe after she's a member of the fam. Like at her wedding, because I need to know this info pronto.

We sit and order drinks. I get strawberry lemonade since it's a special caloric occasion. We have yummy bread and order. I order Mama's trio and a salad.

"Happy birthday, Gert." Heather smiles and hands me an envelope. "I thought you might have fun with this."

I open the card, which is a cute little girl playing dress-up and looking in the mirror. The inside of the card is shiny and framed so I see my wavy reflection in it. It says, "Time Flies." Heather wrote in it, "I wish you the happiest of sixteenth birthdays!" She enclosed gift cards from Sephora for a makeover and a hundred bucks' worth of makeup.

"Oh my God, thank you so much." I hug her. I think I like having Heather in the family. She gives awesome presents.

"It's a special day." She shrugs and smiles.

Mike beams like she's the best thing he's ever seen. It's kinda cute.

"What's Sephora? Am I saying it right?" Mom asks.

See what I mean? "It's a girly store, Mom, with lots of makeup and perfume and fun stuff."

She's puzzled. "Oh. Where is it?"

"There's one at the Plaza."

"We should go, then. Soon." Mom nods. "That's very thoughtful, Heather."

I'm editing the weather talk. The sports talk. The talk about Mike's latest thesis and the new class he's teaching at the college. Mom quizzing Heather about her family and hobbies and whether or not she likes children. Heather teaches preschool, so I'm fairly certain she likes children.

The server clears our table.

Mike hands me a tiny little jeweler's box. "Happy birthday, sis."

"Thanks." I rip open the paper and take the top off. Inside nestles a silver charm bracelet. I pick it up and start checking out the charms. A little car, some keys, a filigree "16," a book, a lipstick, and what looks like a tiny human brain. "Mike, thanks. It's perfect." I turn to Mom and have her put it on my wrist.

"You're welcome. Glad you were born."

All of a sudden the restaurant erupts in loud, boisterous singing. A bunch of servers are coming our way holding a cheesecake with lit candles on it. I think they are singing in Italian. It's not English. The fam joins in when they switch to the English "Happy Birthday."

I look at the cheesecake, completely embarrassed but secretly thrilled by the attention. Clapping.

"Make a wish," Heather whispers to me.

I close my eyes and think about everything I'd hoped turning sixteen would mean. Of course, this is the list I've been compiling since I was eight. So it takes a few minutes.

"Hurry up, Gert, the place will catch on fire." Dad's demand breaks my concentration.

I don't know what to wish. Wish to be cooler and more confident. Prettier. Have a boyfriend. Know all about manliness and how to deal. Get my best friend back. Make friends with more people. Pass my driver's exam. Ace my midterms. Get into the college of my choice, which is still undecided. I don't know. I just jumble them all together and blow.

All sixteen flames flick once, twice, then puff—gone. If I only knew which wish stuck to the smoke, I'd be all set.

As we're leaving, Mike jogs over to his car. "Gert, I've got those books you wanted for school."

He pulls out a brown grocery bag and walks back over. I didn't ask him for any books. But Mike doesn't do things without a reason, so I keep my mouth shut.

He leans down. "Don't show parents the bottom book. The rest you can give back to me the next time I'm at the house."

The parentals don't even notice.

"Love you, Gertie." Mike hugs me. Heather hugs me.

"Thanks for coming." Now I have to get home to see what the secret spy book is at the bottom of the bag. The suspense is killing me.

"Thanks for lunch. I have to go study for midterms," I say, moving toward the stairs.

"They start tomorrow?" Dad asks.

"Yep."

"Get going, then." Dad turns on the television and flips to pro football. It's a Sunday.

I race up to my room and shut the door. I dump the bag on my bed. The very bottom book is wrapped with a 3 × 5 note card stuck to it with tape. It reads: "Thought this might prevent my credit card being used for the next emergency. Happy to discuss anything if you've got questions. Heather also says she'll answer anything. Ask her. —Mike"

The book weighs a ton and is about four inches thick. I have no idea what this could be; it's too big to be a plucking manual. I rip off the paper. *The Guide to Getting It On.* Holy-Mother-of-Birthday-Wishes-Come-True.

I flip through while sinking down onto my bed. It appears comprehensive. I begin reading at random intervals. Holy buttocks, it's all here. I will have no questions go unanswered from this day forward. I will have answers on every topic. I now have answers to questions I didn't know I had.

I glance at the stack of books and notes I must review for midterms. I read a little more of the *Guide*.

I really need to study.

Midterms. Must pass midterms.

I'll just read a little more, then I'll start studying. Soon.

"We still on for Wednesday night?" Adam asks as we exchange hellos running from first period to second.

"Yes. Definitely." We watched *Sixteen Candles* when he turned sixteen. We will watch it again on the eve of my sixteenth. It's been the plan since sixth grade.

"Saturday night. Save it, okay?" Adam demands as we race in opposite directions.

"Fine," I yell over my shoulder. Not like there's anything else beating down the door of my social life. I haven't even seen Stephen today. Maybe he's avoiding me because he thinks I'm a bad kisser. After last night's reading, I'm no longer a technique flunky. I know things.

Last night Adam and I watched *Sixteen Candles*. Rather, I made him watch it with me. It's classic. And well, sad, except for the end, which beats the hell out of my first kiss.

Mom wakes me up a half hour earlier than usual for school. "Come downstairs. I've made us a special breakfast, and you have presents to open."

"Coming." Presents from my parentals are usually whacked. They are not things I necessarily want but things I need. Like new undies, shampoo, a new tooth-brush. Occasionally they score, but it's rare. However, this year Mike and Heather took the pressure off.

"Morning, Sweet Sixteen." Dad kisses my fore-head.

The dining room table is covered with a paper tablecloth, and streamers hang from the light fixture. It's all pink with Barbie on it. It's the thought, right?

I'm wearing black today. Sweater, cords, boots. Black. Mostly to keep my butt from getting all the at-tention on my big day. "Can you put this on for me?" I hand my dad Mike's bracelet to hook for me. I don't quite have the hang of one-handing it.

Mom makes pancakes from a mix, so they're actually not too bad. They're edible. Especially with tons of syrup.

She brings out a huge present wrapped in balloon paper with Disney princesses on it.

My parents sing an off-key birthday song as I tear the paper. It's a new comforter. Navy blue with white piping. "I couldn't buy you black, dear. And this was on sale."

"No, it's great. Thank you." Better than Hello Kitty, but it's going to look like the navy puked on my bed.

"Open this next." Dad hands me a small box with a gold bow on top.

I open the box. It's a brass key chain with my initials engraved on it. "Thanks."

He shrugs and looks embarrassed. Dad doesn't do much with emotion. "We'll get you your own car as soon as you have a license. Nothing fancy. Nothing new."

No, not a new car, but that's expected. I'm just happy they aren't presenting me with a new bike.

"Dear, we've even decided we will pay your insurance through the end of the semester, so you can take your time finding the right job." Mom beams.

"Thanks. Thanks a lot." For not feeling different, the people around me sure are acting different.

"Your driver's test is scheduled for tomorrow at one. I'll pick you up early from school." Dad and Mom hold hands and watch me walk out the door to the bus. I swear they're teary eyed.

I'm feeling rather Disney, until the stench of the bus hits me. Reality check.

There's a white rose in my locker vent. Who put it there?

"Happy birthday." Adam hugs me.

"Did you?" I say, pointing at the locker.

"Nope. Was here when I got here. I've had to guard it, though. Freshman girls are kleptos."

I smell the rose. *Did Stephen? Really?*

"Calc today, right?" Adam asks.

"Yeah, last test." So far so good. If I do okay on the calc exam, I will have passed them all with surfing colors. I have the feeling my 4.0 will stay steady. Thank Holy-Mother-of-College-Apps.

Did my feet touch down today?

Maybe a little. Maybe once or twice.

Maybe.

rants and raves #0
the origins of the notebook
(the beginning)

I've been thinking, Adam's comment about my boring rambling is disconcerting. Okay, so ninety-nine percent of the time I am undoubtedly correct in my assessments, but I don't particularly want to suck Adam's eardrums through his nose in sheer tedium. But I don't want brain explosions either—like with a sneeze that's not let go, what happens when the cork is put in ranting? There could be significant damage, and I'm not willing to take that chance.

I considered posting it all on MySpace or an equally creepy Web site, but who reads those things? Guys in prison and sex offenders, and of course, the producers of shows like <u>Dateline</u>. Not really my target audience. I'd be afraid riots would start at the state penitentiary and I'd have cult followers breaking down my door. I mean, when you're right, there is a bit of responsibility that comes with it.

Not that I really want just anyone reading my rants either. Though profound, I'm sure, they're personal. And Adam's about the only person who gets me. At least I thought he was the only person. Maybe I'm wrong about that. Or maybe he doesn't understand me as much as I'd hoped. Must think on that later.

So no sites, no blogs. I'm not really a graffiti kind of girl and I'd pretty much have to use every wall in the girls' bathroom if I wanted to educate the masses. I'm not ready to join the school newspaper; besides, they'd make me write about stuff that's uninteresting, not only my topics of choice.

I was thinking Adam was doomed to listening as I was pawing through my closet looking for shoes. When, no kidding, just as I was about to stand up the damn unicorn diary hit me on the head. Now, I put it in the back corner of the floor of the closet, so how did it get up high? And why did it choose that moment to bonk me? These are two questions I don't know the answers to, but I'm going out on a limb to suggest divine intervention.

But even at my most benevolent hour, I can't get past the cover with the Proactiv-desperate sheep. Mother Teresa would have chuckled at the sheer ludicrousocity of the unicorn. So I snuck downstairs, grabbed the duct tape and a screwdriver out of the kitchen junk drawer and one of Mom's special scrapbooking markers in silver.

With serious masking, the diary slowly turned into a gray, textured book of emptiness. I pried off the lock with the screwdriver, leaving only a small hole that was easily covered with the duct tape. There's nothing I can do about the pink floral-scented pages, but at least now the tome no longer screams Disney.

I finished with its makeover but was still vaguely unsatisfied. It needed a name. A title. If I'm seriously going to write down my thoughts, then I want to know who I'm talking to.

I don't want a "Diary." Lameness.

"Journal" sounds like I need to be drinking carrot juice and dancing naked at the solstice.

"Dream catcher" implies I dream of things worth writing down, when in reality I get giant dancing penises.

"The Rambler." Wasn't that a Kenny Rogers song before my time, or a John Wayne movie? Neither makes me feel delightful.

"The Ranter." No.

"Ranting." I don't just say negative stuff, though, so that's all confusing.

"Raving" implies lunatic.

"Rants and Raves." That's it. With the sparkly pen I wrote in huge letters across the cover, "The Rants and Raves of Gert Garibaldi." Mine. Me. Perfect. Have to say, it's working so far. No more comments from Adam, and no brain explosions.

nineteen

I am Dario Franchitti, the race car driver, married to Ashley Judd. Now that I think about it, I'd rather be Ashley. I am one with my vehicle. I am the engine. I am the speedometer. I am the revving doohickey.

"Any idea why people are so nervous when they take this part of the exam?" The driving instructor won't shut up. He keeps pestering me with questions and inane conversation.

"Nope, but maybe there's just a lot of pressure," I answer, turning the wheel slightly to avoid a bug. I hate it when they splat on the windshield.

"Are you sure you don't have any suggestions about how to get kids to relax? They'd sure do a better job driving if they stopped trying so hard."

I grip the wheel tighter. If he'd just shut up, I'm trying to drive.

"Turn right."

I spin the wheel a little too enthusiastically. Crap, I should have turned into the outside lane instead of the inside one.

He marks on the clipboard from hell. "Turn right here again, please." He smudges at the window.

I hit the signal. But I don't look over my shoulder. Crapping buttocks, he's making me nervous.

He writes again. "So, can you shed light on the whole thing for me?" He won't take the hint and leave me alone.

"Well. Um. Maybe they're trying to pass," I say with a death grip on ten and two. Think and drive? Is he insane? Conversation is so not going to happen. There's traffic. Lots of traffic. Why are all these people driving now? Couldn't they go a different way?

"Go ahead and parallel park here." He won't take his beady eyes off the cars and trees around us.

I can do this. I can do this.

Orange cones outline a parking space to pull into. They are really quite close together. I pull up, reverse, turn the wheel and flinch. "Those orange cones aren't important, are they?" I ask. I'm hoping he doesn't notice they are crushed beneath the rear wheels.

He sort of looks at me. I can't tell what he's thinking. "Go ahead and drive us back to the DMV." Does he seem paler? A little shaken?

Sweat dribbles down my spine. It's itchy and distracting.

He doesn't talk to me the entire drive back to the department. I'm trying not to count up all the mistakes I'm sure I made. I put the parking brake on. Turn off the ignition. Silence is excruciating. He keeps writing on the clipboard. Pulls out his calculator. Taps his pencil. I can see my parents peering out the DMV window watching for me.

"So, Miss Garibaldi, I'm sure you realize that wasn't quite up to par on overall driving ability."

I hang my head. I can't even unbuckle my seat belt. *I'm a failure. I don't deserve to be sixteen. I don't deserve to—*

"If it was up to me, I would want you to have a little more practice before giving you a license. However, we go by a point system, and you, Miss Garibaldi, have exactly the minimum points needed to pass."

It takes a moment to hear him. I'm stuck on the "more practice" part of his monologue.

"I passed?" I shake myself. "Really?"

"Barely. And with trepidation." He doesn't look like he thinks I've given his words enough gravity.

"But I passed?" Just to be clear.

"Yes, Miss Garibaldi. If you'll come back inside, we'll get your license printed out for you. But, please, be careful for the next several months as you get used to the experience."

"Yeah, sure." I passed. I really truly passed.

Adam's throwing me a surprise party at the burger place. He's so not good at secrets. I'm sure the whole gang and then some will be there. Maggie. Tim. Clarice and Spenser. Stephen. Victor and Greg. A new kid named Jesse and his little sister. Maggie really likes him.

I shower my newly drivable body. I moisturize and pedicure and I'm ready. Oh, and clothes. I put on a casual black dress with newly purchased red and black Skechers. My charm bracelet and huge silver and black dangly earrings. Gloss on the lips. Mascara on the lashes. Powder for the face.

I'm driving to my party. I. Am. Driving. To. My. Party. Oo, that's got a nice ring to it.

I bound downstairs, where Dad is standing waiting for me. "Keys to the car. I put them on your key chain for you."

"Thanks." I can't stop smiling.

"Drive carefully. Slowly. With caution."

"Yep." I am caution personified.

"Have fun, dear, and be home by midnight." Mom kisses my cheek and hands me a black leather minibag I borrowed from her months ago. "I made sure the insurance information and a Triple-A card are in your wallet."

I don't point out the overkill on Gert-getting-into-an-accident preparedness. "Thanks." I restrain the skipping urge on the way to the car.

Keys? Check.

Mirrors? Check.

Minty gum for fresh breath? Check.

Mom is trying not to be too obvious with the curtain peeking. She'd be dead in two minutes as a CIA operative.

I got the lecture last night about the parking brake and the no radio and the no friends in the car. I get it. I really get it.

I turn the ignition. Release the brake. Back up into the street. Where did that trash can come from? Brushed it. Not even a scratch.

I'm doing it. I'm driving. By myself.

I flip on the radio. Turn it up mega-loud and sing along to the latest pop song about teen love gone wrong. Oops. Hallmark card moment over. I probably should have stopped at that light. Nobody sees. I think.

I walk into the burger place expecting Adam and a huge crowd. It's just Adam. He's waiting for me inside the door. I try to nonchalantly look around him for the gynormous "Surprise!"

Nothing. Zilch.

No balloons. No loud music. No clowns making balloon animals.

"Hi." Adam holds the door for me.

"Hi." I want to ask so bad it's killing me. What

happened to my plan he'd throw me a party for my sixteenth birthday? I have reminded him every year since my thirteenth birthday. He can't have forgotten.

"You want fries or a burger, too?"

"Um." *What?* "Fries."

"Drink?"

"Coke." I can't believe it. It's just a normal Saturday night.

"I'm buying, birthday girl, you sure that's all you want?"

"Yeah." My party is nonexistent? *Okay, shake out of it. You're disappointed, but you wanted more time with Adam, just the two of you. Here it is. Make the best of it. Get over yourself.*

I do shake out of it. We talk like we haven't in ages and Adam is so great about actually giving me the boy perspective on the erection question. He even helps me understand Stephen a little more.

We have a perfect time together. Just like it used to be. Perfect.

"Want a coffee? I kinda want a caramel swirl thingy," Adam says as we walk out about nine.

"Sure. I don't have to be home for a couple of hours still. Where's Tim tonight?"

"He had plans."

We amble toward Starbucks. "This is good." I tuck my hand through his arm.

"Yeah, this is," Adam agrees, leaning into me. We do the silly Laverne and Shirley sidestep walk. "I had the funniest thought the other day. Do you remember how you used to beg me to throw you a surprise party for your sweet sixteen?"

"Yeah. I remember."

"That was so funny. I can't imagine you of all people liking a surprise party. I almost did it just to call your bluff, but I figured you'd hate me."

"No worries. This is better." I'm genuinely happy right now. In this moment I feel perfect. Pretty. Smart. Funny. Like I'll make a good adult and I can stop worrying so much about the little stuff.

Adam pulls open the Starbucks door. "You didn't think I'd do it at the burger place, did you?"

I glance at Adam as the entire Starbucks erupts into "SURPRISE!"

I laugh and clap my hands. "You did. You did."

"Of course I did. That's what best friends are for."

Tim waves and comes over. Everybody is here. People I don't know are here too. It's cool, though.

Clarice and Maggie crowd in for hugs and pats. Stephen hangs back with Spenser and Victor.

I walk over to Stephen. "Thanks for coming."

"You get the rose?" he asks.

"That was you?" I smile. "Thanks. Thanks a lot."

"Happy birthday."

"Thanks."

He pulls me away from the table of presents toward the corner. "I have to ask you something."

"Okay."

"You want to date?"

"Um, well." I'm not sure if he's asking for a specific time or, like, a general exclusivity.

"Just us, dating each other," he says.

"Yeah, that'd be good." I smile and warmth blooms in my heart. My fingers tingle. My first real boyfriend.

He leans in to kiss me, but Clarice pushes me toward the group. "Later make out, cake eat now!" she yells over her shoulder, trying to compete with the loud music.

And there on the table is a cake smeared in black icing with white "Happy Birthday!" and a candle shaped like a red convertible. Adam lights it and everyone screams, "Make a wish!"

I don't wish as I blow out the candle. I think I've gotten my quota of wishes come true this year. I'll leave some for next year.

Adam leans down and whispers in my ear, "Happy sixteenth."

I reply, "It is happy, isn't it?" I smile at my friends, my boyfriend, my best friend, Maggie and Clarice, who've come through for me more than I dared dream when school started. In the back hanging with a group of Pops is Lucas. Even Lucas came to my party.

Okay, here's the deal. This perfect happiness won't last, but as long as I take life one butt cheek at a time, I will survive.

About the Author

Amber Kizer is not one of those authors who wrote complete books at the age of three and always knew she wanted to be a writer. She merely enjoyed reading until a health challenge that began in college forced her to start living outside the box. After one writing workshop, she fell in love with telling stories; a million pages of prose later she still loves it. Her characters tend to be opinionated, outspoken, and stubborn—she has no idea where that comes from.

A food lover, she plans trips around menus, wishes cookbooks were scratch and sniff, and loves to make complicated recipes—especially desserts. When she's not reading from a huge stack, she's coaxing rosebushes to blossom, watching delightful teen angst on television, or quilting with more joy than skill. She takes her tea black, her custard frozen, and her men witty. She lives in the Seattle area on a veritable Noah's Ark: a pair of dogs, a pair of cats, fifteen pairs of chickens, and uncounted pairs of shoes—without the big boat and only some of the rain.

A celebrated speaker and teacher, Amber gives writing workshops for all ages. For more information about Amber, for a list of appearances, or to request a school visit, please see www.AmberKizer.com. For more from Gert, including deleted scenes, original material, and sneak peeks of upcoming Rants and Raves, visit www.OneButtCheek.com.